THE ACADEMY OF LOVE series:

"[A] pitch perfect Regency …. Readers will be hooked. " (THE MUSIC OF LOVE)

★*Publishers Weekly STARRED REVIEW*

"An offbeat story that offers unexpected twists on a familiar setup."

(A FIGURE OF LOVE)

Kirkus

"[A] consistently entertaining read."

(A FIGURE OF LOVE)

Kirkus

Praise for THE MASQUERADERS series:

"Lovers of historical romance will be hooked on this twisty story of revenge, redemption, and reversal of fortunes."

Publishers Weekly, STARRED review of THE FOOTMAN.

"Fans will be delighted."

Publishers Weekly on THE POSTILION

Praise for Minerva Spencer's *REBELS OF THE TON* series:

NOTORIOUS

★A *PopSugar* Best New Romance of November

"A remarkably resourceful heroine who can more than hold her own against any character invented by best-selling Bertrice Small, a suavely sophisticated hero with sex appeal to spare, and a cascade of lushly detailed love scenes give Spencer's dazzling debut its deliciously fun retro flavor."

★*Booklist STARRED REVIEW*

"Readers will love this lusty and unusual marriage of convenience story."

NYT Bestselling Author MADELINE HUNTER

"Smart, witty, graceful, sensual, elegant and gritty all at once. It has all of the meticulous attention to detail I love in Georgette Heyer, BUT WITH SEX!"

RITA-Award Winning Author JEFFE KENNEDY

More books by S.M. LaViolette & Minerva Spencer

Minerva's OUTCASTS SERIES

DANGEROUS

BARBAROUS

SCANDALOUS

THE REBELS OF THE *TON:*

NOTORIOUS

OUTRAGEOUS

INFAMOUS

THE SEDUCERS:

MELISSA AND THE VICAR

JOSS AND THE COUNTESS

HUGO AND THE MAIDEN

THE ACADEMY OF LOVE:

THE MUSIC OF LOVE

A FIGURE OF LOVE

A PORTRAIT OF LOVE

THE LANGUAGE OF LOVE

DANCING WITH LOVE

A STORY OF LOVE*

THE MASQUERADERS:

THE FOOTMAN

THE POSTILION

THE BASTARD

THE BELLAMY SISTERS

PHOEBE

HYACINTH

SELINA*

THE BACHELORS OF BOND STREET:

A SECOND CHANCE FOR LOVE (A NOVELLA)

ANTHOLOGIES:

THE ARRANGEMENT

THE WILD WOMEN OF WHITECHAPEL

THE BOXING BARONESS

THE DUELING DUCHESS*

THE CUTTHROAT COUNTESS*

Audacious

Minerva Spencer

writing as

S.M. LAVIOLETTE

Crooked
Sixpence
CS
P
Press

CROOKED SIXPENCE BOOKS are published by

CROOKED SIXPENCE PRESS

2 State Road 230

El Prado, NM 87529

First printing March 2023

10 9 8 7 6 5 4 3 2 1

Printed in the United States of America

Chapter 1

Eastbourne

December 14, 1832

I f Antonia hadn't looked at Lucas "O Duque" Cruz at exactly that moment, she never would have seen the expression that flashed across his face: a look of yearning so profound that it rocked her to her core.

He wants me.

The thought exploded in her mind with all the subtlety of a pyrotechnic display at Vauxhall Gardens, and her eyes locked with Lucas's.

For one soul-shakingly intense moment he stared at her as if he wanted to *consume* her, his dark eyes blazing, the muscles beneath his skin taut with desire.

And then, right before her eyes, his gaze shuttered and all that desire disappeared.

No, a voice inside Toni's head amended. *It's not gone; it's just hidden.*

Impassive once more, Lucas turned away and nodded at something Toni's mother, Baroness Ramsay, said, his harsh features relaxed and cool, not as if he'd just looked at Toni with enough heat to set her on fire.

"Is aught amiss, Toni?"

She jolted at the sound of Marcus's—Lord Stanford—question, and hastily composed her startled features into a polite smile.

"I was just pondering what you said," she lied, scrambling madly to recall what he'd been talking about.

Mark smiled. "You are always such a good listener."

Toni's face heated yet again, this time with shame rather than excitement.

"Give the matter some thought," Mark went on, "And you can tell me what you decide next week when I return from London."

"Of course," she said, hoping he'd forget *the matter* by then. Toni adored Mark and they'd been friends since they were babies, but lately he'd developed the most inconvenient infatuation for her and followed her around like a needy puppy. She knew that she should dissuade him, but she also knew how agonizing it was to suffer an unrequited longing for somebody.

Or at least she'd believed her feelings were unrequited until a few seconds ago. Had Lucas really looked at her that way? Or had it been wishful thinking on her part? Or perhaps a trick of the light?

"Let me take those to the wagon," Mark said, once again jolting Toni from her fugue.

"Hmm?" she murmured.

Mark gestured to the stack of pine boughs.

"Oh, of course. I'll help you," Toni said.

They gathered up two armloads and carried them toward the already enormous pile of pine cuttings that would be used to make garlands to decorate her family's ancestral home, Lessing Hall.

Christmas was usually her favorite holiday, but this year Toni was finding it difficult to get in the festive spirit. She had already begged off the sled races earlier that day, so she'd known that her family would think something was wrong if she hadn't come tonight.

So, here she was, marking time with one suitor while gazing at another.

You only wish that Lucas was your suitor.

Toni scowled at the unwanted, but true, thought. Lucas Cruz—the fearsome privateer that she and her siblings had always called Uncle Duke—was also her father's best friend and the man she'd secretly been in love with for four long, miserable years.

"Look!" Mark said, pointing at something over her shoulder. "First star tonight, Toni." He grinned at her. "Make a wish."

Well, that was easy. Toni made the same wish she'd been making for years: *I wish Lucas was mine.*

She sighed and turned away.

"It didn't take you long to decide what to wish for," Mark said in a teasing voice. "You must want something badly. I don't suppose you would share your wish with me?" He smiled up at her, a hopeful glint in his attractive blue eyes.

Ugh. She really needed to sit Mark down and put an end to his unrealistic hopes.

But not tonight; not at her family's Christmas party.

"If I tell you, then it won't come true," Toni said lightly.

Mark chuckled. "Fair enough. Why don't you come warm your hands by the fire? They must be frozen." He gestured to three big braziers set up around the pavilion,

"That would be lovely," Toni said. Not because her hands were cold, but because it gave her a better view of Lucas.

"May I fetch you hot chocolate and something to eat?"

Toni wasn't hungry, but she really needed a few moments alone. "Yes, thank you, Mark."

Mark moved toward the huge, colorful cloth tent that shielded an immense table, groaning with every sort of delicacy imaginable. Along the way, he stopped to say hello to some of the other guests that had come for the annual tradition.

Toni's family—especially her father, Baron Hugh Redvers—was mad about Christmas and the yearly collection of evergreen boughs and mistletoe had become an activity that many people in the area looked forward to. There were over sixty guests—most of them younger people, friends of Toni and her brothers—combing the wooded area, looking for mistletoe and trimming off branches to use for garlands. Of course, the actual point of the evening for many of her unmarried friends was the opportunity to flirt and get up to mischief while roaming the small, wooded area.

That is what Toni should have been doing—sneaking kisses and cuddles with a lover, which is certainly what Mark had in mind. Instead, she'd purposely stayed near the pavilion, where the older people had clustered around the fires to chat, just so she could gaze on the object of her infatuation.

Obsession would be more accurate, a dry voice mocked.

No, that wasn't right, either.

Unfortunately, the way she felt about her father's closest friend wasn't anything as harmless as infatuation or obsession. It was a far, far more dangerous emotion; it was love, and it had bubbled inside her for years, like a cauldron that was constantly on the brink of boiling over.

Even before she'd fallen in love with Lucas, she had loved him.

At first, it had been the innocent love a child felt toward an adult who made them feel safe and cherished. Lucas was her favorite uncle—although they were not actually related by blood—and Toni had always regretted that he only came to Eastbourne twice a year and his visits were always far too brief.

Lucas had been a part of her life for as long as she'd been alive, one of the three men her father trusted most in the world and the person to whom Hugh Redvers had finally sold his beloved ship the *Batavia's Ghost*.

Although her father and Lucas had both retired from privateering, people still spoke of both men in awed whispers. One-Eyed Standish and O Duque—the Portuguese raider people called The Duke—had captured more slaver vessels than any other ship to sail beneath His Majesty's colors.

Lucas wasn't just a favorite with Toni, but with all six of the Redvers siblings and they'd looked forward to 'Uncle Duke's' visits because of the exciting, exotic stories he told, the wonderful gifts he brought, and the way he always made a point of spending time with each of them on his biannual visits.

5

While Toni treasured the gifts he'd given her over the years—unusual items that he collected on his journeys around the globe—it was his company that she had always looked forward to most.

At least that had been true until the year she turned sixteen, when Toni had fallen wildly, intensely, and—yes, hopelessly—in love with Lucas Cruz.

Even at such a young age, she had known her love for Lucas was hopeless and that he would never, ever think of her the way she thought about him.

To Lucas, Toni would always be the daughter of his dear friend, a little girl he'd known since birth, who called him *Uncle Duke*. How could he—a feared privateer with a lifetime of experience—possibly fall in love with somebody as unworldly and immature as Toni?

Lucas's visit that November had been both heaven and hell. Heaven because Toni had spent time with him—as she always did—and hell because instead of being his card partner or sailing with him in his yawl, accompanied by her younger brothers, Toni had wanted him all to herself.

She'd been both relieved and miserable when Lucas had sailed away at the end of his stay, the six months between that visit and the next an eternity.

Toni had known that she had to make a choice. She could either try to stamp out her emotions for Lucas or she could say something to him on his next visit.

She'd opted for the former and had spent the six months between his visits throwing herself into the country entertainments that abounded around Eastbourne. Although Toni hadn't fallen in love with any of the dozen young men who'd sought her out at the myriad balls and country assemblies, she'd gained confidence and polish, crossing that invisible line between girlhood and womanhood.

By the time Lucas returned to Eastbourne, Toni had convinced herself that she'd finally cut him out of her heart.

It had taken only one look at his rugged, beloved face to smash her hopes to flinders; if anything, she'd loved him more than ever.

Toni should have confronted him at that point—although what she would have said she still didn't know—instead, she had suffered in silence through another visit where he'd treated her like a child.

And when he'd sailed away again, Toni had been left with a constant ache in her chest, as if she were missing a vital organ.

It was at that point that she'd accepted the truth: she could not bear to be there the next time Lucas came to Eastbourne. It was too exhausting to hide her love, and it hurt too much to be around him when he treated her like a little girl. The best thing she could do was stay away from him and hope her feelings faded with enough time and distance.

So, Toni had begged her parents to allow her to make her debut a year early. Despite some misgivings about her age—she'd only been seventeen at the time—they had reluctantly agreed.

And then, at the end of the Season, they had grudgingly permitted her to attend a house party rather than returning home.

"But if you go to this party, you will miss your Uncle Duke's June visit and I know how much you enjoy seeing him," her mother had argued.

Toni could hardly tell the baroness that missing Lucas's visit was the reason she'd asked for a wretched London Season to begin with.

Nor could Toni tell her that she couldn't bear sharing meals with him or socializing with him or—worst of all— watching him board his ship at the end of his brief visit and sail out of her life for another six months.

And she especially couldn't tell her mother that it was no longer possible for her to pretend that she thought of Lucas as her *Uncle Duke,* not when she'd had dreams so vivid it made her blush just to recall them.

No, Toni said none of that to her mother.

Instead, she'd said, "Please, Mama, everyone is going to this house party; even the Duke of Dowden will be there."

Her parents—who'd never denied her any reasonable request, and plenty of *un*reasonable ones—had allowed her to go, even though she knew they didn't especially care for Dowden.

And so, Toni had not seen Lucas that June.

By the time late November rolled around that year, Toni had been betrothed to Dowden and had remained in London until Lucas's visit had passed on the pretext of preparing for her wedding, which was to take place at Lessing Hall that Christmas.

And what a disastrous Christmas that had been...

After the debacle with the Duke of Dowden, Toni had been too ashamed to look Lucas in the eyes and she'd leapt at her parents' offer to tour the Continent for two years.

All in all, Toni had avoided Lucas's visits for four long years, until she simply couldn't bear it any longer.

She had hoped and prayed that her love for him had dissipated over the years, but it had only taken ten seconds in his presence to prove she'd been a fool. Once again, Toni found him more handsome and charismatic than ever.

The first three weeks of this visit had been agony. She'd wanted to be around him, but she'd also been afraid that she would inadvertently expose her feelings.

Even more agonizing was the fact that there was only one more week remaining in his stay and she had scarcely spoken a word to him

Instead, she'd engaged in surreptitious *Lucas-watching*. Toni couldn't help worrying that her strange behavior was being noticed, if not by her parents—they both appeared as unconcerned as ever—then perhaps by the object of her love and obsession.

In fact, Toni *knew* Lucas had noticed her reserve because there had been a quizzical look in his whiskey brown eyes when he'd given her the gift he'd brought this year, a bolt of sea-green silk so fine that it had felt like a warm summer breeze on her skin.

Lucas had never brought her anything so… intimate, something she would wear against her body.

Toni had tried not to read too much into the gift, but after the look she'd intercepted a few moments ago perhaps—

She brutally cut off that hopeful train of thought. It had only been *one* look. Just one. She needed more. She needed proof.

Her eyes settled on Lucas, who was no longer in the larger group, but was standing off to one side with her father. Toni couldn't help noticing that her father, who was normally smiling and gregarious, was scowling.

Whatever he said must have made Lucas scowl.

And then both men turned and looked at Toni—as if she were the topic of their conversation.

She ignored her father and stared at Lucas.

For the second time in less than ten minutes, raw hunger blazed in his eyes.

He quickly turned away, but she'd seen the look and was not mistaken. He *wanted* her.

The joy that surged in her chest was so intense it made it difficult to breathe. There was something else, too: hope.

But that hope was tempered by reality. Because regardless of Lucas's yearning looks, Toni knew that if anything was going to come of the attraction between the two of them, then *she* would have to make the first move.

***

"I wish you'd stay longer this year, Duke," Hugh said, not for the first time that week, or even that day. "It is the first Christmas in years that all my children and their families—not to mention Bouchard and Delacroix—will be here. Who knows when that will happen again?"

"I will consider it," Lucas lied, lowering his head to take a sip of his drink and cutting a fleeting glance toward the far side of the fire and the reason that he should not extend his stay: Hugh's only daughter, Antonia.

Lucas swallowed down his desire and wrenched his gaze away, so ashamed of his thoughts that he could not look Hugh in the eye.

Hugh Redvers wasn't only his closest friend, he was also the reason that Lucas was among the living.

Lucas had been eleven years old when his entire Portuguese village was captured by corsair marauders. Because he'd been exceptionally large for his age the slavers had kept him on as a rower while selling the rest of his family. He'd spent two of the most miserable years of his life chained to an oar before Hugh seized the corsair vessel and freed Lucas and a dozen other captives.

Hugh hadn't just rescued him from a short, brutish life of slavery. He'd also taken Lucas under his wing afterward and taught him a valuable trade. Lucas had started out as a cabin lad and worked his way up, until he captained one of Hugh's three ships.

And then, seven years ago, Hugh did something Lucas had never expected: he offered to sell him the *Batavia's Ghost*.

"There is no other man who deserves her more than you, Duke," Hugh had said.

"But what of Delacroix or Bouchard?" Lucas had protested, naming the two other men who'd captained the famous vessel before acquiring ships of their own.

"They both agree with me," Hugh had assured him.

Lucas had never come so close to weeping in the presence of another person in his life. That Hugh, Jean Delacroix, and Martin Bouchard—the three men he respected most in the world—would think him worthy of owning the

Batavia's Ghost touched him more than anything he could recall.

After Lucas had taken charge of the ship, he probably should have changed his home port to somewhere other than Eastbourne—somewhere more convenient—but he had not wanted to lose the connection with Hugh and his ever-increasing family.

Hugh had been a father, brother, and best friend to him since the day he'd rescued him almost thirty years ago. Not only had Hugh freed him and made him wealthy, but he'd taught Lucas to read and write and to manage the fortune that he'd acquired over the years.

Lucas owed Hugh *everything*.

And Lucas had repaid all Hugh had done for him by lusting after his only daughter.

Just thinking about Antonia Redvers made his eyes slide toward her... *again*, but he checked himself before he could complete his search. Looking at Antonia was something he tried to limit himself to doing only once an hour, not that he could ever exercise such restraint.

Usually, Lucas was lucky if he glanced at her less than ten times an hour, which was why he had tried to keep his distance from her on this visit. No more riding around the estate with her; no more taking her sailing on his yawl; no more admiring her sketches or her archery—just *no more.*

Lucas took a sip of his drink and was struggling to keep his gaze from Antonia when he saw Hugh was staring in that same direction, his normally smiling face uncharacteristically stern.

If Hugh was staring at her, then surely Lucas could risk a glance?

So he allowed himself to follow his friend's look.

He scowled at what he saw: a stripling named Lord Marcus Stanhope—a friend of the family—was standing beside Antonia and gazing down at her with his heart in his eyes. The boy had been following her everywhere during this recent visit.

Just looking at the mooning, lovesick lad was enough to make Lucas feel more than a little violent.

At least he's not old enough to be her father, a cruel inner voice taunted.

The taunt—something he'd dealt with for years—had not lost its sharp edge. Even if Lucas could forgive himself for desiring Hugh's pride and joy—which wasn't likely—he could not forgive himself for being attracted to a female so much younger than himself. Hell, she was young enough to be his daughter!

As if Antonia could feel the crushing pressure of his yearning, her pale green eyes locked with his.

Heat exploded in his body—centered in his groin—the reaction so feverish and intense that it boded ill for getting any sleep that night.

Antonia's expression was so somber that Lucas's heart ached for her. Her smile used to illuminate any room she occupied, but something had dimmed her light. She was so very different than she'd been almost four years ago—the last time he'd seen her. She wasn't just older and even more beautiful; she was also a woman who had loved and lost.

"He is undoubtedly in love with her, but I cannot like such a match for Toni," Hugh said.

Lucas startled at the sound of his friend's low, unhappy voice and swallowed down the lump that had appeared in his throat at the other man's words. "Er, you mean Antonia is betrothed to Stanhope?"

"No, not yet, but I fear an announcement is imminent, as he has been a constant visitor ever since Toni returned home a few months ago."

"You don't like him?"

"He is a nice young lad, it's just... well, I do not think he is right for her."

"Is there something wrong with him—like the last time? What was her betrothed's name?" Lucas asked, even though the name was branded into his very soul.

Hugh scowled. "No, thank God, young Stanford is nothing at all like the Duke of Dowden. Antonia was *extremely* fortunate to escape marriage with that vile scoundrel." He leaned closer to Lucas. "I never told you what Dowden did, did I?"

"You didn't," Lucas said. "But I assumed it was something reprehensible if you needed to take Antonia away for two years after the betrothal fell apart."

"It was worse than reprehensible; it was criminal. Toni discovered Dowden wasn't just a philanderer, he is also a rapist and blackmailer."

"Good God, Hugh! Did he touch her or—"

"No, no," Hugh hastened to say, "he never laid a hand on Toni, thankfully, but he forced himself on one of our servants— a sweet young woman who grew up playing with our children and whose family has worked for mine for generations. Luckily, the girl had a lover who stood by her and they're now married with two children." He grimaced. "The oldest child is the result of Dowden's assault."

Lucas squeezed his glass until his knuckles whitened. "This Dowden sounds like the sort of *porco* who needs to be taught a lesson, Hugh." It enraged him to think of such a scoundrel getting anywhere close to Antonia Redvers, a young woman who was as close to perfection as any of God's creations.

Hugh grinned—the nasty, blood-thirsty grin of One-Eyed Standish, the fearsome privateer, rather than Hugh the loving friend and father. "Never fear, Duke. I've taken steps to ensure Dowden is an extremely unhappy—and tractable—man."

"What did you do?"

"I bought all his debts and then threatened to call them in if he so much as *thought* about marrying any other young woman or if I heard even a whiff of scandal about him. In addition, news of his behavior somehow leaked out." Hugh's smirk deepened, leaving no doubt who caused that *leak*. "Dowden is now something of a pariah, regardless of his grand title."

Lucas snorted. "Money and shame? Bah! I was thinking of a different sort of punishment—one that involves my fists and his body."

"Thrashing a duke will land you in leg irons, my friend."

"I would be long gone from the country before they can arrest me. Is the *filho da mãe* in London or at some country estate? I could pay him a visit after I attend to my business in Tunbridge Wells next week and—"

15

"*No*, Lucas. She is mine to protect, and I have done so," Hugh said, his face hard and stern. "I do not need anyone else to avenge my daughter."

Lucas knew that when Hugh used his given name rather than his nickname that he was serious.

He ground his teeth, aware that the other man was right. *Hugh* was her father while Lucas was nothing to Antonia—not a blood relative or anyone of substance—with no right to fight for her honor.

"I want you to promise me you won't act on your anger," Hugh persisted.

"Fine. If you insist."

"I'm afraid I must. I'd hate to stir the entire matter up all over again. I just want Toni to move on and forget about it all."

"Do you think she has moved on? Or is her heart still broken?"

"That is the odd thing, Duke. I don't think she ever loved him."

"And yet she abandoned society after their betrothal fell apart?"

"Yes, but I think her confidence suffered a greater blow than her heart ever did."

"What do you mean?"

"Just that Toni is so upset with herself for not noticing what a snake Dowden was that she is afraid to trust herself."

"How could she possibly have guessed such a thing? Four years ago, she was just a child—innocent and trusting." Lucas hesitated and then said something that had been sticking in his craw for years. "I could not believe that you and Daphne would give your consent to such a betrothal."

"You mean because of the age difference?"

"She was only seventeen, and he was—what? Why are you laughing?"

"Have you forgotten that my wife was once married to my uncle, Duke?"

"No, of course I haven't forgotten that. But I cannot see what—"

"My uncle was over three times Daphne's age and she and I are more than a decade apart," Hugh went on. "We would be hypocritical if we'd tried to forbid Toni's marriage because of the gap in their ages—which was fifteen years, by the way. It wasn't the age difference that concerned us so much as Dowden's character. Even before I learned he was a rapist, I knew he had no intention of discharging his mistress when he married Toni." He scowled. "You must know how I feel about that sort of thing, especially for my daughter."

It was true that Hugh was intensely loyal to his wife. Lucas had always been impressed that a man who'd once kept mistresses in every port had settled into monogamy so quickly and happily.

"Why do you think she accepted such a man?" Lucas asked, giving voice to a question that had kept him awake far too many nights.

"I don't know," Hugh admitted. "Her mother and I have pondered that a great deal. Toni has never been interested in grand titles and she does not need to marry for money—not that Dowden had any. He is accounted to be a very handsome man, if one can look past the fact that something is off about him."

Hugh shook his head. "I daresay I will never know Toni's reasons for accepting the man. In any case, it was a painful, but important lesson that she learned."

"What? That men can be pigs?"

Hugh snorted. "Well, that, too. But I meant that nature sometimes hides the most evil, dangerous predators in the most attractive packages."

It was Lucas's turn to snort. The same certainly could not be said for him. Even his mother, God rest her soul, had teased that Lucas would need to be a magnificent lover to attract a wife because no woman would love him for his appearance alone.

Lucas had not been a handsome lad and now he was grizzled, scarred, and possessed more than a few gray hairs. He was no woman's dream lover, especially not a sensitive, beautiful young woman like Antonia.

Indeed, the thought of a man like him—with his huge meaty hands and massive, brutish body—touching an exquisite goddess like Antonia Redvers was enough to revolt even him.

But God, how he wanted her!

Lucas realized he was once again staring at her while she chatted happily with the eligible young man beside her and wrenched his gaze away, turning back to her father.

Hugh was looking at him with an odd expression that sent a spike of fear through his chest; had the other man guessed at Lucas's thoughts?

"What is it?" he asked.

Hugh seemed to shake himself and the smile he gave Lucas was a rueful rather than murderous one. "I'm hoping that

Toni doesn't settle for young Stanford just because he is safe, present, and persistent."

Lucas swallowed down the bile that rose in his throat at the thought of another man touching her. "Perhaps she is in love with him?"

"No, she is not in love."

"How can you be sure?" he asked, even though he knew he was treading on dangerous ground.

But once again, Hugh was too concerned with Antonia to notice Lucas's preoccupation with his daughter. "Because Toni is just like me." Hugh suddenly grinned. "I'm sure you can remember what I was like when I met her mother."

Lucas couldn't help laughing. "I recall you were, erm, visibly besotted."

Hugh threw back his head and gave one of his bellows of laughter. "That's putting it mildly. Delacroix teased me so damned badly I almost lashed him to an anchor and tossed him into the Channel," Hugh admitted with a chuckle. "Toni is the same; when she falls in love, everyone will know it." Hugh was both proud and confident as he looked across the room at his beautiful daughter.

Lucas knew it was unwise, but he allowed himself one more peek at the woman who had long ago captured his heart.

This time, Antonia was staring back at him, her expression strange—almost knowing.

Lucas jerked his gaze away. Bloody hell! He hoped to God that she never guessed the lewd, lustful, yearning thoughts that he felt for her.

Chapter 2

L ucas sat back in his chair, heaved a sigh of contentment, and sipped his fine brandy.

It had been a long, busy, tedious day—filled with a series of meetings with solicitors, his man of business, his tailor, and bootmaker—and he was glad it was over for another six months, until the next time he returned to England.

He was exhausted by so much talking, but he was pleased to have his banking business out of the way. It seemed the more money a man accumulated, the more time he had to spend managing it. Which he supposed made sense, but he could do without the long, boring conversations with bankers who loved nothing more than to talk, talk, talk about money.

He'd also taken the opportunity to get fitted for a new pair of boots that afternoon. The bootmaker in Tunbridge Wells had been making his footwear for almost twenty years, and today the man's son—a lad of nineteen—had taken Lucas's measurements. That had brought home to him, yet again, how inappropriate his emotions for Antonia Redvers were. Even if she wasn't the daughter of his best friend, at only twenty-one, she was far too young for him.

Lucas snorted at the irony of it all; he had waited all his life to fall in love and then he'd gone and fallen in love with the wrong woman.

Oh, he'd had plenty of lovers over the years and he had even been tempted to settle down a time or two. But the temptation had always passed. Like most sailors, he kept mistresses in more than one port of call, but the number of women had dwindled over the years as most of his lovers had married and settled down.

Lucas had been at sea for three decades and the itinerant life of a sailor no longer held the same attraction for him as it once had, and yet it was difficult to imagine a life on land after all this time.

After Hugh had freed him from bondage, Lucas had embraced his life at sea because it had allowed him to search for his family.

But over the years, he'd found nothing but disappointment. First, he'd discovered his mother had died in Cairo only two years after they'd all been captured.

Then he'd learned that his younger brother had died three years after that, when the ship he'd crewed on had gone down in a storm.

Lucas's three older sisters had disappeared into the flesh markets of Oran, and no amount of searching had turned up a single clue as to their whereabouts.

Seven years ago—after twenty years of searching for Maria, Ana, and Sofia—he had given up. The guilt he'd felt at the decision had been crushing, but the trail, if there ever had been one, had become so cold as to be nonexistent.

His only family was Hugh, Delacroix, and Bouchard. But all three men had married and now had proper families of their own.

Lucas knew he should stop coming to Eastbourne; he should make this visit his last—at least until he heard Antonia was safely married. It would be painful to stay away, but it would be worse if—

"Can I bring you another glass of brandy, Captain Cruz?" the waiter asked, thankfully interrupting his painful musing.

"No, this will be all for me, thank you." Lucas tossed back the last of his drink, heaved himself up, and made his way to his room, which was two floors above. The Norwich was the nicest hotel in Tunbridge Wells and he'd stayed there every year for at least a decade.

Just a few streets over was a brothel—also the nicest in the city—where he'd spent many an entertaining evening during his dull business visits.

But not tonight.

Tonight, he was unaccountably... sad; his stay in Eastbourne was almost over.

As he trudged up the two flights of stairs, he seriously considered leaving early. What was the point? As much as he loved seeing Hugh and the rest of his family, it was simply too painful. His unease had obviously transmitted itself to Antonia given how she'd taken to avoiding him, and they'd barely exchanged two words.

There had been a time, not too long ago, when Antonia had thrown her arms around him when he'd arrived, when she had come out to the ship, along with her brothers, and poked into the treasures he'd transported to England from exotic ports around the globe.

This visit she hadn't even come to the ship, and she'd been uncharacteristically quiet in the evenings when the boisterous Redvers clan met in the sitting room to play card games or charades.

More and more, Lucas worried if she sensed something from him—that he'd not kept a tight enough grip on his emotions—that made her reticent and uncomfortable.

He unlocked the door to his suite of rooms, which was the largest in the hotel. Because he spent most of his time onboard a ship and in a small cabin, he enjoyed the luxury of space when he had the chance.

The maid had come and gone while he'd been at dinner and the fire was crackling merrily in the sitting room hearth and the port he liked was on the end table beside the comfortable wing chair.

Lucas had purchased several books today and was especially looking forward to reading *Ivanhoe,* which the clerk at the shop had enthusiastically recommended. He'd not learned how to read until later in life, so it was still a great luxury to stroll into a bookstore and actually be able to peruse books.

He poured himself a glass of port, pulled off his neckcloth, and then collapsed in the overstuffed wing chair.

Only after he opened the book did he recall that he'd left his reading glasses on his dressing table that morning. He could read without them, but he'd found that he developed a headache, so it was better to look like an old man than to have a sore head. Especially when there was no danger of anyone seeing him.

He sighed, pushed himself out of the comfortable chair, and strode toward the door that connected the two rooms.

Lucas was reaching for his glasses when his gaze fell on a valise beside the dressing table. He frowned; that wasn't *his* valise.

He stared at it for a moment, his mind sorting through possibilities and discarding them until he settled on one: a hotel servant must have delivered the bag to the wrong room. There was probably an unhappy guest wondering what had become of their luggage.

He'd have to ring the bell for somebody to come fetch it.

He strode toward the bellpull beside the bed when he noticed the body sprawled out over the counterpane.

A *female* body.

Golden-red hair had come loose from its moorings and spilled across the pillow, obscuring the woman's face.

It was a shade of hair that only two people he knew possessed.

Blood thundering in his ears, Lucas reached out and brushed a lock of hair back—as if he really needed to verify his suspicion—and gasped at the sight of her beautiful, sleeping face.

"Antonia! What in the name of God are you doing in my room?"

Chapter 3

Antonia?" A hand lightly shook her shoulder.

Toni smiled at the sound of the familiar voice. Ah, it was going to be one of *those* dreams.

"Antonia?"

"No," she muttered, pulling away from the hand, not wanting to wake up.

"*Antonia.*"

Yes, that was definitely the raspy, accented voice Toni adored, but never had it spoken her name so… roughly.

Almost as if he were *angry*.

The startling thought yanked her from her pleasant doze and Toni opened her eyes to see the face of the man she thought about day and night.

She waited for the delightful image to dissolve around the edges and disappear like it always did.

But this time, it… didn't.

Indeed, his face became less fuzzy the longer she stared.

"Lucas?" she whispered, and then blushed wildly when she realized it was the first time she'd ever called him anything other than Uncle Duke.

Rather than look surprised by her informal address, he looked… thunderous. "What on earth are you doing here, Antonia?"

Had his voice always sounded so very stern?

His black brows plunged even lower. "Answer me," he barked.

His commanding tone sent a ripple of emotions through Toni's body, most of them completely inappropriate to the anger in his voice and the harsh glare in his usually soft brown eyes.

"Er, I came to see you," Toni said, her brain too sluggish to be more articulate.

The muscles in his jaw flexed and his eyes flickered over her, as if he might find an answer somewhere on her person. He looked ferocious—frightening, even. The only thing that kept her from being terrified was the way his thumb was absently, and oh-so-lightly—stroking her temple, as if he'd forgotten that he was touching her.

He yanked his hand away as if she had scorched him and hastened away from the bed, not stopping until he was near the doorway.

He crossed his powerful arms, his frown deepening. "How did you get here?"

Toni took a moment to admire his magnificent physique.

She was five feet eleven inches in her stockinged feet and had to look up a little to meet his gaze, which was not something she had to do often with members of the opposite sex.

While he was nowhere close to as tall as her father—at six and a half feet Hugh Redvers was the tallest man she had ever seen—Lucas was still two inches over six feet.

If he wasn't the tallest man she'd ever seen, he was certainly one of the broadest. His shoulders were massive and filled the doorway almost as completely as the door.

Tonight, he was wearing his evening clothes and the muscles in his thighs and biceps flexed enticingly beneath the fine wool.

Although he wasn't handsome in a classical sense, he was so intensely masculine that he seemed to charge the surrounding air. His sensuality—that was the word for it, Toni was sure of it—filled her lungs when she was near him, intoxicating her.

At night, in her bed, she closed her eyes and imagined that mouth on her body, those scarred, brutish-looking hands exploring, claiming, and dominating her. He would be gentle, but strong. She just knew it.

And because he was a man, and not a boy, he would know how to pleasure a woman. Somehow, Toni knew that, too, even though the most she'd ever done was kiss a man, barely a peck on the lips.

The Duke of Dowden—for all his many faults—had never tried to do more, a fact which had annoyed her at the time, but now made her very grateful.

"Antonia!" he snapped.

She jolted. "What?"

"I asked you a question. How did you get here?"

Rather than bristle at his commanding tone, a warm, sensual wave of desire pulsed through her, as if honey, rather than blood, coursed through her veins. He'd always had that effect on her, but tonight, it was more intense. Her breasts felt heavier, her nipples hard and sensitive against her snug bodice.

Toni realized he was glaring and shook herself. *A question? He asked me a question. Now what was it again?*

Oh, yes: how had she come to be in his rooms?

"I rode here on Wicus."

"You rode all that way alone!"

"I'm not made of glass, Lucas."

He winced. "You should not call me that."

"Why not? It's your name, isn't it?"

His throat flexed as he swallowed. And then swallowed again. "It—well, it makes you seem grown up." His tanned cheeks darkened even more.

"I am twenty-one years old, Lucas, and as *grown* as I shall ever get."

His eyes flickered over her as they had when he'd woken her, but slower this time, his nostrils flaring slightly and his enormous chest rising and falling faster.

Toni reveled in these silent signs that he wanted her—that he found her attractive. If only he didn't look so… grim about the matter.

"You need to get off that bed," he snapped.

"Why? What is—"

"Antonia."

It was only one word, but his tone was so stern that it caused a delicious fluttering in her belly.

"Fine," she said.

Once she'd slid off the bed, he gestured to the sitting room. "Come sit by the fire."

Toni chose the settee, hoping that he'd sit beside her. Instead, he leaned against the wall, as far from her as the room permitted, as if she were some sort of wild animal and he needed to keep his distance.

"Where do your parents think you are?"

"Visiting a friend in the next village."

"They let you ride to the next village alone?" he demanded, openly skeptical.

She shrugged rather than admit that she usually took her groom with her.

He groaned and briefly closed his eyes, as if he didn't need her answer. "Antonia, what in the world are you thinking of coming here?"

Toni hadn't envisioned her audacious plan feeling quite so awkward when she'd conceived of it. Truthfully, she hadn't considered his reaction much at all—it had been too worrisome to imagine what he would do, especially when all the evidence pointed to him being shocked by her behavior.

Which is exactly what he was: shocked.

Remember those heated looks he gave you, Toni? He wants you, even if he isn't showing it.

That was a mantra she'd needed to repeat incessantly over the past two days.

Unfortunately, Lucas appeared so forbidding right now that it was all too easy to believe that she'd imagined his hungry looks.

But she hadn't. She *knew* she hadn't.

Toni squared her shoulders and reached deep within herself for courage. "I came here because I thought we might, er… "

"Yes?" he prodded, his confusion making his harsh features somehow… adorable. "You thought what?"

It was the curiosity and vulnerability in his dark gaze that emboldened her. "I thought we could stay here for a few days. Um, together."

His lips parted, but no words came out.

The silence was excruciating.

"I—I came here because I thought you wanted me," Toni blurted.

His thick black eyebrows pulled down into a V over his high-bridged nose. "I beg your pardon?" he asked in a higher-than-normal voice.

Strangely, now that Toni had said it once, it didn't seem so difficult. "I thought you wanted me—as a man wants a woman."

Lucas stared for perhaps a decade before muttering, "Good God." He strode across the room and then back before shoving a hand through his curly black hair, clearly at a loss for words.

His reaction was crushing, but Toni took comfort in the way his hand shook just a little. That slight reaction, coupled

with his wild-eyed confusion, made her braver. "I want you…
Lucas."

"*You* want *me*," he repeated in a flat voice.

"Why do you sound so shocked?" she asked, mildly
offended that he thought so little of himself. Or perhaps he
thought Toni was too much of a little girl to know what *wanting*
meant?

"Because I am old enough to be your father—older than
old enough." He gave a snort of disbelief. "Because I am your
father's friend. Because I am a sailor. Because I am the son of a
whore—pick a reason."

She flinched at the word *whore*, which she'd never heard
spoken aloud before.

He muttered something beneath his breath that sounded
like a few of the Arabic words that her father used from time to
time and then said, "I am sorry, Antonia. I should not have
spoken so in your presence."

Toni bristled at his apology. "Why? Because women
aren't supposed to know about wh-whores even though many
women *are* whores?"

Lucas didn't look half as startled by her words as she felt.
She'd *never* said anything so wicked in front of a man before.

It actually felt… good.

He inhaled deeply, his already massive chest seeming to
double, and then exhaled slowly. "Antonia, this"—he gestured
between them— "can never happen."

His words hurt more than she'd thought they would, even
though she'd expected them. "You don't want me?"

He briefly squeezed his eyes shut and when he opened them again, he said. "It's not about wanting. It's about—"

"That is *all* it is about, Lucas—two adults wanting each other. I have already declared my interest in you. If you don't want me, just tell me and I shan't bother you again. I will feel like a fool, but it will be better than not—"

A frustrated noise tore from his throat. "My God, Antonia! I want you more than I've ever wanted any other woman in my life."

Toni blinked. "You—you *do*?"

"Yes. But that doesn't matter. Can you imagine what you father would say if he knew you were sitting here in this room with me? Can you?"

Toni could easily imagine her intimidating and overprotective father's response to this scene.

"He would be… upset," she admitted.

"*Upset*?" he gave a strangled laugh. "I speak four languages and I don't think any of them have a word to express what your father would feel if he could see us right now. Have you seen that sword that hangs in his study?"

Toni scowled, not liking where this conversation was going. Not liking it at *all*.

She crossed her arms. "Of course I've seen it," she said tightly, feeling any chance of happiness slipping from her grasp. "It is difficult not to notice a six-foot broadsword."

The weapon in question was the sort that had been used several centuries earlier, but she knew her father had employed it more than once when he'd been One-Eyed Standish.

"He would kill me, Antonia. And you know what?" Lucas asked, not waiting for an answer. "I would deserve killing if I ever put these"—he lifted his huge hands— "anywhere near you. You are precious to him, the most precious thing on earth. To Hugh, you will always be his baby girl."

Toni sprang to her feet, suddenly furious. "I am not a *thing*, Lucas, nor am I an infant; I am a woman grown. I was betrothed to a man who was almost twenty years older than me, and my father did not complain." That was a fib. Her mother and father had been ambivalent about their age gap—among other things—but they had not forbidden the match.

"The man was a duke, Antonia, which is a great deal different from the captain of a ship."

Toni was tempted to point out that Lucas was known around the world as *O Duque,* but she suspected he was not in the mood for teasing.

Instead, she said, "But you are an honorable man and my father's best friend—surely that would matter to him?"

"You are the daughter of a great aristocratic house, Antonia. I come from nothing and could never fit into your world. I know you know that."

"I do know that," Toni admitted. "But do you really think that is what I want—to live among the haute ton? If that was the case, then why have I avoided London for the last three years?"

"Because you were hurt by your experience with Dowden. But you will eventually forget about him and go back to the world where you belong. One day, you will find a man you want to spend your life with."

"I have already found such a man."

Lucas stared, his coffee brown gaze darker than usual. After a long moment, he sighed, dissipating the strange, charged atmosphere that had built up between them.

"What I meant is that you would eventually find somebody appropriate to love, Antonia."

"Am I not allowed to choose who I love?"

"Of course you are. I did not mean—"

"Then I choose *you,* Lucas. You are the one, and you *have been* the one since I was sixteen. Actually, I probably loved you before then, but that was the first time I wanted you as a woman wants a man. I have been in love with you for years."

Disbelief, joy, more disbelief, and then anger flickered across his harsh features. "And yet you were betrothed to another man."

The bitter—and yes, jealous—words stunned Toni. They also fed the tiny flame of hope that still flickered inside her.

But before she could speak, he groaned. "I should not have said that. It is none of my—"

"I am relieved that you mentioned my betrothal to Dowden, Lucas, because it allows me to explain something. I accepted his offer because I knew how it would be with you— what you would say if I ever gathered the courage to confront you with my feelings. I knew you'd never listen to me."

Toni took a shaky breath and plunged onward. "For an entire year after I recognized my feelings for you, I struggled with the choices I faced. Finally, after living through two of your visits, not to mention the many months in between when I missed you so badly it was physically painful, I concluded that too much stood between us—my father, my age, our differing statuses—that it was pointless to want what I could not have. I decided I would find a man I could respect and live with—even if I didn't love him—and try to banish you from my heart." She forced herself to look him in the eyes. "I made a dreadful muddle when I chose Dowden and I was fortunate to escape a lifetime of misery. I know how lucky I was."

Toni gave him a chance to speak.

When he remained silent, she went on, "After that fiasco with Dowden I thought to myself: why marry at all? It is such a risk for a woman to trust her life to a man—as Dowden had proven—that it simply wasn't worth it. Why not live alone? After all, I don't *need* to marry; my father has made sure I have enough money for a life of luxury. A husband and children are not the only reason for a woman's existence—both my parents have taught me that."

She shrugged. "So, I threw myself into my other interests—especially helping my older brother manage the restorations taking place at Lessing Hall—and that was *almost* enough, Lucas. And then you showed up for your bi-annual visit and I realized, yet again, just how hollow life was without you."

Lucas opened his mouth—probably to apologize for visiting or say something horrid like he would never visit again, or both.

But Toni didn't let him speak. "You met my Great Aunt Amelia, didn't you?"

He frowned at the change in direction but nodded. "Yes, I recall her." A slight smile pulled at his full, shapely lips—his one truly beautiful feature. "Hugh delighted in forcing me and Martin Bouchard to eat dinner with her back when your father returned to England. I understand she died last year?"

"Yes, she was ninety-nine. Aunt Amelia never married, never had a family, and lived at Lessing Hall all her life."

"Hugh told me there was some scandal when she was a girl?"

"Yes, it happened when she was only eighteen," Toni said. "After my debacle with Dowden, my Great Aunt Amelia sent for me. She told me a story about when she had been eighteen years old and had fallen in love with a man whom her brother, the Earl of Davenport—who'd been her guardian at the time—forbade her to marry. The earl claimed that my aunt's beloved was a fortune hunter after her money and that was why he wouldn't allow them to marry. My aunt was devastated and unable to finish her first and only Season. Not long after my uncle brought Aunt Amelia back home, the man she'd been in love with married another woman—an heiress."

"So then your great uncle was right; he *was* a fortune hunter."

"Yes, my uncle was right and my Aunt Amelia admitted that. But she also made an excellent point: just because her lover married for money did not mean that he would not also *love* his wife."

Lucas drew in a breath, as if to say something, but let it out and nodded without speaking.

"My aunt always believed that she would have been happy if she'd been allowed to marry him," Toni said. "Whether she would have been, nobody will ever know because she wasn't given the chance to find out. But I know this, Lucas: Aunt Amelia wasn't happy living her life alone. Although she adjusted to her solitary existence, she never stopped being lonely, and she never forgot about the man she loved. It is tragic that my aunt never had a chance for happiness." Toni's eyes suddenly burned with tears. "And I'm terrified that the same thing might happen to me."

Their eyes locked and Toni struggled to read his expression. Did he know what she was saying? Did he feel the same way, or had she just imagined it all and was making a dreadful fool of herself?

As much as she wanted to ask him those questions, it was Lucas's turn to speak. If he wanted her, he needed to at least meet her half-way.

Chapter 4

L ady Amelia Redvers's story was heart-wrenching, especially as Lucas knew the old lady and it had been clear that she was not only deeply unhappy, but more than a little mad.

While Lucas had not known the cause of Lady Amelia's unhappiness until tonight, it did not surprise him to learn that it was love.

Indeed, he had felt more than a little mad himself ever since the year when Antonia and Jonathan had come to the *Batavia's Ghost* one afternoon and he'd been astounded by the changes that had occurred in his best friend's daughter since his last visit only six months before.

Lucas had long been accustomed to Hugh's children making themselves comfortable on the infamous old ship. Before Antonia and Jonathan, there had been their older brothers, the twins Lucien and Richard, who'd treated him as their favorite uncle.

Lucas loved all Hugh and Lady Ramsay's children, but there had always been something special about Antonia, and not only because she was Hugh's only daughter.

"I still recall the first time I saw you," Lucas said. "You were so small and fierce and your father was so proud of you he could not even look at you without getting emotional." He chuckled softly. "Who would have believed that One-Eyed Standish—one of the most feared men to sail the seven seas—could weep with joy?"

Antonia smiled but did not speak.

"Even when you were little, it was clear that you were your father's daughter, bravely toddling after your two older brothers, infuriated when they refused to take you along on their adventures."

Antonia chuckled, her anxious expression softening at his words. "Lucien and Richard were always such beasts to me. They were like a nation of two," she said, her gaze vague as she looked into the past.

Lucas nodded. "I suspect that special closeness often occurs among twins, but I could see that it made you very lonely. I remember I was relieved when Lady Ramsay had Jonathan a few years later, giving you somebody all your own."

Her lips parted in obvious surprise.

"What?" he asked in a teasing voice. "You think I am too much of an old salt to notice things like that?"

She snorted. "I don't think you are either *old* or *salty*," she said with a tart look that was adorable. "I'm just surprised that you noticed because we saw you so rarely."

"Your family is the closest thing to family that I've had since I was eleven years old. Being your uncle has been one of the joys of my life."

Her green eyes flashed. "But you are *not* my uncle, Lucas."

"No, I am not," he agreed. Lucas took a moment, weighing his next words. He knew it had taken a great deal of courage for Antonia to come all the way to Tunbridge Wells, put herself in a vulnerable position, and then share her feelings.

He owed her the same.

He met her intense gaze, a bittersweet smile twisting his lips. "It is a damned good thing I'm not your Uncle Duke, considering the thoughts I've had about you these past few years."

Her lips parted. "Wh-what thoughts might those be?"

"I recall both my visits during your sixteenth year perfectly," he said, choosing not to answer her question. "That winter I brought the *Ghost* to Eastbourne for extensive repairs."

"You stayed longer than you ever had before. Almost two months," she said.

"You and Jonathan showed up for part of most days to watch." He smiled. "And occasionally you helped, although I must admit it caused me more than a little anxiety when you insisted on climbing the mast."

She laughed, the sound a low, sensual chuckle that was like a punch in the stomach. "You were so shocked when I showed up wearing breeches that day. You didn't believe me when I told you it was my mother's idea."

"The baroness is a surprising woman," he muttered, his unruly mind wandering back to that afternoon—and the way Antonia had looked with her suddenly shapely hips stretching a pair of her brother Jonathan's old buckskins.

He thrust the fetching memory from his mind and whipped his thoughts back into order.

"You and your men have always been very kind to me and all my siblings." Antonia said, clearly not understanding the wicked thoughts she'd unleashed by reminding him of that day.

Lucas gave a noncommittal grunt; he really was the lowest sort of beast to be lusting after her while she was innocently reminiscing.

She gave Lucas a shy smile. "I must admit I was glad that Jonathan was every bit as eager to spend time on the *Ghost* as I was that year. Although we had very different reasons."

The spark of heat in her gaze went straight to Lucas's cock—which was already as heavy and hard as a yard arm—and he shifted uncomfortably in his chair.

"I think I fell in love with you on that very first day of your visit."

Her simple declaration gutted him, and Lucas knew he owed her the truth. "While it wasn't the first day for me—only because I was too startled by how much you had changed—it was probably the second."

Lucas knew it was wrong to enjoy the look of pleasure that bloomed on her beautiful face at his admission. He'd just done something he'd sworn never to do—he'd opened a door that should have always remained closed, locked, and barred.

Good God. He'd just confessed how he'd felt to Hugh's daughter!

He lurched to his feet. "I need something to drink. Would you—"

"I'll have whatever you're having."

"All I have is port. I can ring for tea if you like?"

"Papa lets me drink port with him."

Lucas jolted at her words.

Antonia groaned, her cheeks staining a fetching shade of red. "I probably shouldn't have brought up his name."

"Actually, it is best that I keep Hugh at the forefront of my mind," Lucas muttered, throwing back the glass of port he'd poured less than half an hour ago—and yet a lifetime ago—and then refilling it and a second glass before turning back to Antonia.

She took the port with shaking fingers. "Thank you."

Lucas sat, heaved a sigh, and then continued.

***

Antonia clamped her jaws tightly shut, determined to keep her mouth shut. It had been a near-disaster to mention her father. She'd seen that by the expression of shock on Lucas's face.

"You were always such a bright, vibrant child, the most like Hugh of his children. Not only do you share you father's green eyes and golden-red hair, but you have very similar personalities."

"You mean bossy, opinionated, persistent to the point of insanity?" she blurted. So much for keeping her mouth shut.

Lucas gave a startled bark of laughter. "I suppose you could say that."

"That's certainly what my brothers say," she muttered.

He smiled. "I was so happy for Hugh. He'd lived a hard life and had so little reward until he met your mother. Oh, he'd accrued plenty of wealth," Lucas added, as if Toni might not know what he meant, "but he'd been alone for a very long time." He met her gaze, his own brooding. "We both had."

Excitement and fear swirled in her belly at his sudden intensity. Lucas Cruz was a man who'd been tempered by savage fires; he was no green boy. Given the brutal life that he'd lived, he'd probably never behaved youthfully even when he'd *been* a boy.

"I noticed the changes in you immediately during that visit. You'd always been lovely, but you'd been a child." He swallowed hard enough for her to hear it. "I swear that you'd been a coltish little girl only six months before, and then"—he snapped his fingers and the loud crack made her jolt—"just like that, you were a woman. A very desirable one."

He grabbed his glass, threw the port back in one swallow, and then looked at her, his eyes blazing with something she couldn't quite decipher. "I was appalled by my reaction to you, Antonia. So appalled that I considered leaving the very next day." He snorted bitterly. "But I was glad that I couldn't leave because of the damned repairs. I tried to convince myself that it was natural to appreciate beauty and that I was doing nothing wrong if I only looked and never acted on my attraction to you."

Antonia realized she was holding her breath and let it out slowly and quietly, not wanting to distract him from his fascinating confession.

"I saw how my men responded to you—how they all noticed you—and it helped me to realize that what I felt was a simple animal attraction. I told my men that I'd cut off the hands, feet, and co—" he stopped, blinked, and then said with a blush, "er, privates of anyone who touched you. I gave myself that same speech, arguing that it was how I managed my attraction that would differentiate me from an *actual* animal." He shook his head, as if she'd argued. "But it was extremely difficult to be around you and hide that I wanted you. Over that visit, I avoided your company because it was just too miserable not to touch you." He gave her an unhappy look. "I hoped it went unnoticed."

"Oh, *I* noticed," Toni said. "I was devastated when you and Jonathan took his new boat out and didn't invite me along. And you no longer joined me when I practiced my archery. We were no longer card partners when we played whist." And a dozen other small ways that he'd avoided her—tiny gestures that had left invisible knifelike wounds on her soul.

Lucas opened his mouth, but Toni wasn't finished. "That first visit was bad, but the next one was worse; we barely exchanged a dozen words during your stay and you left a full week early."

He dropped his gaze, his expression contrite. "I'm sorry that I did not handle my attraction maturely." He looked up, his eyes hot like they'd been a few nights earlier at Lessing Hall when she'd caught him staring at her. "I'd never felt such a powerful attraction in my life, and I was unsettled by the intensity of my reaction to you. I'd hoped the feelings would fade during the visit, but I left Lessing Hall more entranced than ever."

Toni took no comfort in knowing that he'd suffered as much as she had. Indeed, it made her feel worse that they'd spent so many years avoiding their own feelings and each other.

"I felt the loss of your friendship keenly," Toni said. "Other than my brothers and father, you're the only man I know who doesn't constantly put me in my place or remind me of my shortcomings. You always seemed so genuinely interested in what I'd been doing, and your gifts reflected the fact that you *listened* to what I liked. Instead of dolls, you had that wonderful bow built for me. Instead of jewelry, you brought me books, puzzles, or those wonderful bongo drums—"

Lucas grinned, the expression rare and brilliant. "Yes, and your mother and father almost banished me for bringing you such a noisemaker."

Toni couldn't help returning his grin. "I actually wrapped it up and will give it to David this year for Christmas."

They shared a laugh at that. David, who at ten years of age was the youngest of the Redvers children, was already shaping up to be the wildest.

Lucas heaved a sigh. "I'm sorry for all the pain I've caused you, Antonia."

"Is it just because of who my father is?" she couldn't help asking. "If I were some stranger's daughter, would you have reacted the same way?"

"I won't deny that is a large—very large—part of it. To a lesser degree, there is our age difference, but more than that is the life that I have led."

"You mean being a sailor? But why would that matter to me? My father was a privateer, after all."

"Your father was a lord before he became a slave, Antonia. There is an immense gulf between us when it comes to social status. And then there is the sort of life that I've lived." His cheeks darkened slightly. "I—well, I've hardly led a saintly existence."

"You mean that you've had many women," she said, proud that she didn't stumble over the words.

He frowned at her question, but nodded and said, "Yes."

His admission heaped fuel on the inferno that flared inside her—the jealousy and envy that had eaten away at her since she'd learned where he sometimes spent his evenings in the small town of Eastbourne. Her brother Jonathan had told her about the women who entertained *visitors* in the large white house behind the Pig and Whistle Inn.

"I know you visit the house behind the inn," she blurted. "I know it's a br-brothel."

His lips parted in shock. "*Bom deus*! How do you know such a thing?"

"Jonathan told me he'd gone to a woman there named Betsy, and that you'd recommended her to him."

The admission left her face hot and doubtless scarlet. But she wasn't the only one blushing. Lucas was the color of a brick, his expression beyond grim.

"I am going to thrash your brother."

"Why? Because he confides in me?"

"Yes! A young woman like you should not be sullied by such matters."

"A young woman like me? How much older than me do you think Betsy is?"

"That is beside the point," he retorted, looking more than a little flustered.

"That is exactly the point, Lucas. Betsy used to play with me, Jonathan, and all the other children in the village when we were younger. She is only two years older than me."

He looked guilty at that information, but his guilt wasn't what Toni wanted.

"You needn't look so mortified. I understand people have physical needs. I may be a v-virgin but that doesn't mean I don't deserve to know the facts of life."

"It is not the sort of thing a young lady should have to know," he retorted doggedly.

"You keep *saying* that! Why not?"

He recoiled at her heated tone, which only made her angrier.

"Why shouldn't I know what the act of physical love is like? Why must I be kept in ignorance when Jonathan—almost two years my junior—not only knows more, but has *done* more? It is a—a—well, it's an injustice, I tell you!"

He opened his mouth, closed it, sighed, and then opened it again and said, "You are right—it seems unjust."

Toni was startled by his sudden capitulation. "Yes, it is," she said rather lamely.

"I must point out that the reason people—er, male people—don't like you to know such things is their desire to protect you, Antonia."

"Or control me."

Again he hesitated, and then he nodded and said, "I daresay there is some of that, as well."

Toni's heart swelled at the way he listened to what she said, never just dismissing her comments out of hand. She hadn't believed that she could love him even more, but clearly, she'd been wrong.

However, they were in the middle of a critical conversation, so she shoved her adoration aside and said, "So you visit Betsy whenever you are in Eastbourne. Do you love her?"

"*What*? No!"

"Why is that so unthinkable? Because she is a prostitute? You think they do not deserve love?"

"Of course, I don't think that. Whores—er, prostitutes—deserve love, too. I told you about my mother, did I not?"

She nodded.

"She raised me and my brother and sisters without the help of a man—I have nothing but respect and honor for her. I only sounded surprised by your question because I would have married Betsy if I loved her."

"So, you would marry a woman you loved, even if she'd once been a prostitute, but you won't marry me because I'm the daughter of your best friend?"

He opened his mouth, but nothing came out. His eyes widened, and then he laughed.

Toni scowled. "Are you laughing at me?"

"No. I am laughing at how quickly you have tied me in a knot." He cocked his head, his smile suddenly the soft, caring expression she was accustomed to seeing on his face. "Is everything so black and white to you, Antonia? Can you not see the reasons I've restrained myself when it comes to you?"

"I know your reasons and—to an extent—understand them. But the other reason so far outweighs your concerns that it should make your decision easy."

"What other reason?"

"How many times have you been in love, Lucas?"

He stared at her for a long moment before saying, "Lust—I have felt many times. What I feel for you? Only once."

Toni wanted to leap up from her chair and shout *huzzah* as her brothers were prone to doing.

But Lucas wasn't finished. "I love your father, too, Antonia; I owe him my life. Several times over, in fact. If not for Hugh, I would have died chained to an oar. Can you even understand the debt I owe him? Not that I view that my gratitude as a burden," he hastily added. "Indeed, it is an honor. And to act on my feelings for you would be to violate that honor."

"So, you will throw away what we might have for honor?"

"I—that is not—" He flung up his hands in a very gallic gesture. "You do not understand."

"Then *make* me." Toni stood up and he shot to his feet almost as swiftly as her shadow. "I love you, Lucas. And yet what you are telling me is that my love doesn't matter as much as *honor*. What you are telling me is that I will live out my days alone because of abstract notions of *honor*. Thanks to *honor* I can move into my great aunt's quarters and spend the rest of my days in mourning."

"You know that is not what I am saying." He gave an exasperated huff. "I want—more than anything—for you to be happy."

"You say that is what you want, but you don't want it badly enough to do something about it. You care for me—you admitted as much—and yet you would throw all that away and condemn us both to a loveless future."

Lucas was large and stocky but he moved with the swiftness of an active, physical man who spent his days on his feet. One moment he was glaring at her from ten feet away, the next his big hands were crushing her upper arms in a painful grip, his pupils huge and dark as they glared into her eyes.

"Do you think I make such a decision easily?" The cords in his neck were as taut and distinct as the thick ropes that ran from the masts of his ship. "What I feel for you is like a fever, a raw, consuming fire in my belly." His eyes dropped to her mouth and his chest swelled as he filled his lungs with air. "I imagine the things I would do to you if you were mine and I'm ashamed by the images that fill my head, Antonia. I am *ashamed* and yet I can't make myself stop thinking about you."

"Tell me those thoughts… *please.*" She suddenly needed to know what he imagined more than she'd needed anything in her life—more than sunshine and food and even air. "Tell me, Lucas. I need—"

His low, animal sound of pure frustration was the only warning she had before his mouth crushed hers.

Chapter 5

L ucas had never been an especially articulate man. Hugh had always talked circles around him—and had enjoyed doing so often on the long sea journeys they'd spent together—and it seemed Hugh's daughter possessed the same skill.

Antonia was like one of those sprites or faeries in the mythology stories he enjoyed so much, luring him toward certain ruin and he was powerless to stop himself from following her.

He wasn't a man of letters or genius; he was a man of action. And so he acted, claiming her plush, bee-stung lips with a savage, starving kiss.

Her sweet mouth opened to his greedy plundering; she was even more delicious than he'd imagined—sweet and fresh and immediately addictive.

She whimpered beneath him, reminding him of the cruel way he was holding her upper arms.

Lucas released her and tried to step away—to apologize for his brutishness—but her hands snaked around his neck and drew him even closer.

He could tell that she had never been kissed before and her efforts were innocent yet eager.

His hands developed minds of their own—greedy, hungry minds that would not be denied—and he spanned her slender waist, his thumbs resting on her prominent hipbones, which he caressed lightly over the multiple layers of clothing.

Antonia shivered at his stroking and pushed her hips toward him, unknowingly rubbing her mound against his aching cock.

He groaned, desperate to move his hand lower, to cup her sex, and slide a finger between her lower lips and—

Lucas, what are you doing? his better angel demanded.

"Caramba!" he hissed, yanking his hands back before he acted on his lustful urges.

You've waited for this for almost four years! his other, far more self-interested devil urged. Touch her! Explore her! Sate the gnawing hunger you've suffered for years.

Lucas stood frozen with uncertainty, desire and honor warring inside him.

And then Antonia's tongue delicately probed his mouth and his restraint shattered.

This time he slid his hands to her lower back rather than her too tempting front, only to encounter even more temptation when his palms came to rest on the firm globes of her arse.

Lucas groaned. "My God, you feel so good," he said, the words coming out in Portuguese, as they often did when he was tired or distracted or aroused. He squeezed her full buttocks and flexed his hips, grinding his aching cock into the sweet notch of her sex. They fit together as if they had been designed for each

other, her height making her the most perfect a
embraced.

arm'

She kissed him as if she wanted to cons
plunging into him with her eager, questing ton;
everything he offered.

"Lucas," she whispered against his lips, nipping and
licking and sucking while pulling him tighter and grinding her
body against his.

His body shook—as if he were feverish. He simply
couldn't get close enough; he wanted—no, he needed—to get
inside her.

Lucas's eyes fluttered shut as he imagined how it would
feel to plunge his cock deeply into her tight heat, her willowy
body bucking beneath him as he stroked into her, filling and
stretching her, her long legs wrapping around him as he pumped
her full of his seed.

His imagination galloped ahead of their coupling, leading
him to some sun-filled future where they were married. Lucas
imagined the results of their love—Antonia's belly swelling with
their child, a golden-haired, green-eyed daughter who would
look just like her.

And just like Hugh.

Hugh.

The thought was like a bucket of icy water over his head
and Lucas's body went rigid—every part of him, not just his
cock—at just how close he'd come to bending Hugh's only
daughter over the back of the settee and mounting her.

Good God.

Lucas took her by the waist and firmly put her body at length, ignoring her whimpers and protests and the way r lips clung to his, the way her hands refused to relinquish his hair.

The pain of having his hair ripped from the roots anchored him even more firmly and coldly to reality.

"Antonia," he said, his voice a hoarse rasp.

Her heavy eyelids lifted slowly, her gaze confused and sullen as her hands slid from his hair. "Why did you—"

Lucas stepped back, putting even more space between them. "We cannot do this." He wiped his mouth with the back of his shaking hand, as if he could wipe away his guilt.

She drew herself up to her full height, for once, resembling her mother rather than her father. "You mean you won't do this."

"Very well. You are right—I won't do this." He swallowed and gestured to the bedchamber. "Use the bed and I will sleep out here. In the morning, I will take you back to Lessing Hall and—"

"You won't take me anywhere, Lucas. I'm not a—a package to be transported from one point to another. An inanimate object with no will of its own." She spun on her heel and strode toward the door that led to the hallway.

"Where are you going?"

"That's none of your concern."

Lucas reached the door before she could get it halfway open and closed it easily, even as she yanked on the handle.

Antonia whirled on him, the crack of her palm on his cheek hard enough to snap his head back. "Step aside and let me out. I am leaving."

"No, you are not. It is dark. You are alone, and far from home without an attendant."

Lucas saw the second slap coming but did nothing to stop it. Why bother? A slap from Antonia was better than a kiss from any other woman. He was fully aware of how that desperate thought made him a sad wreck of a man, but he just didn't care.

Her eyes blazed when he did nothing to defend himself. "You can stop things tonight, but tomorrow I am going to tell my mother and father that I love you."

Joy and terror leapt inside him at her words. Could she sway her father on such a matter? Would her love be enough to make Hugh accept such an unworthy man for his only daughter?

You are a fool to even imagine such a thing. Would you want to have you *for a son-in-law if Antonia were your daughter?* a bitter voice in his head mocked.

He was a fool.

Lucas met her furious green gaze. "You must do what you feel is necessary, Antonia. And I will also do what I think is necessary."

"And what do you mean by that, pray? That you will run away and never come back?"

He felt shame at her accusation, but he couldn't deny it. He would run from his oldest friend's anger just like a coward.

"Yes, that is exactly what I will do."

Her fury drained from her body as quickly as it had flared and she swayed.

Lucas took her shoulders. "Steady," he murmured. "Do you feel faint?"

"No. Not faint," she said, her voice lifeless, her green eyes hazed with pain and hopelessness.

"Will you stay in my chambers and let me take you home?"

"Yes. I'll stay here. You have my word that I won't sneak out," she said when he hesitated.

He nodded, and she turned away, her shoulders slipping from his grasp.

"I'll never speak of this to my mother or father or anyone. Ever." She threw the words over her shoulder and then closed the door behind her.

Lucas slumped against the wall, gutted and confused by her sudden capitulation.

She had listened to reason, and he had won.

So why did he feel as if he'd lost?

Chapter 6

They left the hotel before first light the next morning.

Neither of them exchanged anything other than the barest pleasantries from the moment Toni woke up alone in Lucas's bed until the moment he lifted her up onto her horse when they were only a few miles from Lessing Hall, his powerful hands burning through the clothing between them and branding her. Toni had felt the echoes of his touch for hours.

But now, five days later, she felt nothing.

Although Lucas didn't leave early as she'd believed he would—at least he'd said nothing about that to her parents—he'd stopped joining the family for dinner, games, and holiday festivities. Toni knew he still saw her father, but the two men always met late in the evening or aboard the *Ghost*.

Toni told herself she was glad he was staying away; she just wanted him to be gone already. This would be the last time she saw him because she would not be at Lessing Hall if he came for another visit.

She hadn't decided where she would go; she could do that later. There would be six long months before she had to find somewhere else to live.

"Are you ready to dress for dinner, Miss Antonia?"

Toni jolted and looked up from the book that she had not been reading.

"I'm sorry; I didn't mean to startle you," Jane, her lady's maid, said, smiling at her from the dressing room door. "I suppose you must have been engrossed in your book."

Toni hadn't turned a page in at least an hour. She couldn't even remember what the book was.

Jane chattered on as she dressed her hair and prepared her for dinner, but Toni didn't hear a word. She kept wondering if she shouldn't just send a message to her mother that she wasn't feeling well. But that would bring its own headache because the baroness would want to send for Doctor Carson.

And so, Toni tolerated Jane's primping and then made her way down to the dining room at the appointed hour.

Dinner was a loud, raucous affair. Her older brother Richard and his wife Celia and their three children were the last of the family arrivals, and now her entire family—all five of Toni's brothers—were home. There were also at least twenty neighbors, and the huge dining room was full of family and friends. Thankfully, Lucas was seated at the far end of the table. Since that last morning—when he'd sent her home on Wicus, a few miles away from Lessing Hall—she hadn't exchanged ten words with him.

The meal felt interminable, and all Toni wanted was to go back to her chambers, curl up in bed, and pull the blankets over her head. Unfortunately, there were games to be played after dinner and then an impromptu dance. Thankfully, Lucas left before the dancing commenced.

By the time Toni escaped to her bed, it was well after midnight.

Instead of falling into a deep, dreamless sleep, she tossed and turned.

Finally, at one o'clock, she could take it no more.

What she needed was a book that wasn't *The Hunchback of Notre Dame*. Although the book was fascinating, reading in French was simply more than her overtaxed brain could manage just then.

What she needed was a comfort read.

Toni shoved her feet into her battered slippers, tied on her flannel dressing gown, and made her way to the library.

When she opened the door to the library, she discovered it wasn't empty.

Her mother looked up from whatever she was reading and smiled at Toni. "Can't sleep?"

"Not for lack of trying," Toni said, going to stand in front of the fireplace. Lessing Hall was a lovely home, but it was always cold. "What is keeping you awake, Mama?"

"I need to finish this paper before Christmas and several points have been eluding me." She put a marker in her book and set it aside. "What about you, Antonia? You've been… distracted these past few weeks."

Toni settled onto the settee across from the baroness and carefully considered her next words. She wouldn't tell her mother the truth, of course, but now might be the time to broach the idea of going away after Christmas—and staying away.

"I'm a little distracted," she finally said.

"I see. And is it because of Lucas?"

"Wh-what?"

Her mother laughed softly. "I suppose I deserve that look," she said wryly. "I know I appear to have my head in the clouds, but I do pay attention to my children." The humor drained from her sky-blue eyes. "I especially notice when any of you are suffering. And you have done so for far too long, Antonia. You needn't pretend with me, my dear. You love him, don't you?"

"How—how did you know?" Toni choked out, startled to feel a tear slide down her cheek. "Oh drat," she muttered, dashing away the drop with the heel of her hand. "I don't know what's wrong with me."

"Oh, darling." The baroness came to sit beside Toni on the settee, wrapping a slender but strong arm around her shoulders.

Toni gave herself up to the comfort of her mother's arms and released the tears she'd been holding inside her since that night in Tunbridge Wells, when she'd slept alone in Lucas's bed with him only in the other room, although he might as well have been on the moon.

"Tell me about it," her mother murmured.

Toni let it all pour out—her illicit journey to Tunbridge Wells, ambushing Lucas in his room, the substance of their disagreement, and her solitary night and journey home afterward.

When she was finished, she felt exhausted but strangely light, as if she'd shed several stone.

"Is your love for Lucas the reason you accepted Dowden's offer of marriage?" her mother asked.

"Yes, but how did you guess?"

The baroness smiled. "It sounds like something I might have done."

"Really?" Toni asked. "But you are always so… logical."

"Not when it comes to love, my dear. None of us are." She sighed. "You've been carrying around a great weight for a very long time, Antonia. I should have done something when you became betrothed. I knew—"

"Please," Toni said, setting a hand over her mother's. "Don't blame yourself, Mama. I can wish that I had never met Dowden or I can choose to regard the episode as a learning event. I've decided to do the latter. After all, as painful as it was, it made me brave enough to tell Lucas that I love him." She snorted bitterly, "For all the good it has done. But at least I can take comfort in the fact that I have done all I could."

One of her mother's pale blond eyebrows lifted. "Are you sure you've done *everything*?"

Toni frowned. "What do you mean?"

A slow, wicked smile spread across her mother's usually serious face, making her look mischievous and girlish. "I mean, my dear, that sometimes with men a woman needs to take the burden of making decisions from their hands. Entirely."

Chapter 7

L ucas heaved a sigh of relief when the *Batavia's Ghost* sailed with the evening tide.

For the last twenty-four hours, he'd worried that something would prevent him from sneaking away like the cowardly rat that he was.

"I don't understand why you refuse to stay for Christmas this year—it is only six days away. What difference will a six-day delay make at this point?" Hugh had asked when Lucas had gone to his friend yesterday afternoon after having decided to leave Eastbourne—and Antonia—early.

"I'm sorry, Hugh, but my passenger has paid a great deal to leave as soon as possible," he'd lied. "You know how people can be."

Hugh had sighed but nodded. "Yes, I do know, which is why I never carried passengers on the Ghost when I was her captain. But that is neither here nor there. I won't interfere with your business."

"Thank you for understanding. Will you pass along my regrets to the baroness and your family for me?"

Hugh's brows had knitted. "You can tell them yourself tonight at dinner."

"I can't, Hugh. I have—well, you know better than anyone how much needs doing before one can sail. And I have so little time to prepare," he'd finished lamely, struggling to meet his oldest friend's suspicious gaze.

"Is something wrong, Duke?"

"No, of course not," he'd protested, forcing a false-sounding laugh. "You've just forgotten all the tasks that need doing—being a gentleman of leisure as you are."

Hugh had chuckled, although he'd looked less than convinced by Lucas's excuses. "I won't pester you any more on the matter. You must do what you feel is best."

Lucas had escaped his friend's house soon afterward, sickened by his deception.

But one thing he'd said had been the truth, and that was the amount of work that needed to be done before they could weigh anchor. He'd been busy until well after midnight and had slept only a few hours, waking at dawn that morning to get an early start on the last-minute preparations.

It had surprised him that none of Hugh's family had come to say goodbye, but he'd told himself to be grateful that there'd been no awkward questions or farewells before he'd departed.

Only after Lucas had listened to his first mate's report and taken the wheel for an hour—enjoying the quiet as most of the crew went below to eat their evening meal—did he allow himself to think about the fact that he wouldn't see Antonia again. At least not for some years. He was determined to stay away from Eastbourne; now that Hugh's son, Jonathan, no longer crewed for him, there was no reason that Lucas couldn't do the right thing and leave her alone.

"Shall I relieve you, sir?"

Lucas turned at the sound of his first mate's voice. "Do I look that tired, Mr. Brown?" he teased, a yawn interrupting the last word.

Brown, a small, wiry man who'd been with Lucas for four years, smiled, his gaze flickering over Lucas's bare shoulders. "Actually, I thought even you must be getting cold, Captain."

Lucas glanced at his bare arms and then at the other man's heavy wool coat and laughed. "I suppose it has become a bit chilly." He had always run hot but wearing only his leather jerkin—no matter how thick—in December was extreme, even for him. "Yes, take the wheel for me, Brown. I probably won't come out again until morning." After all, he could stew in his cabin far more comfortably than he could on deck.

"Good night, sir."

Lucas looked forward to stretching out on the oversized bed—courtesy of Hugh from the days when he'd been captain of the Ghost—and relaxing in his cozy, warm cabin, which was the only one on the ship that had a stove other than the galley. Again, that was a holdover from the days when Hugh had been captain, as the big man was always cold. Lucas mainly used it to fight the constant damp, but on a night like tonight, the warmth would be welcome, too.

He nodded at several sailors as he passed the galley on the way to his quarters.

"Captain?"

He stopped at the sound of his cook's voice. "Yes, Jones?"

"Earlier I sent the kitchen lad to light your stove, but your cabin was locked, sir."

"Locked?"

"Yes, sir."

Lucas frowned; he rarely locked his cabin unless he went ashore.

"Shall I send the boy to light it now?" Jones asked.

"No, I won't have a fire tonight." All he really wanted was some sleep.

When Lucas reached his cabin, he slid the small brass key into the lock and turned it until he heard the tumbler click.

The first thing he noticed was the lamp next to the door, which he'd not left burning.

The second thing he noticed was a small cloth bag sitting on top of the charts and papers cluttering his desk.

And the third thing he noticed was the beautiful young woman sitting on his bed.

Garbed only in one of his shirts.

Lucas quickly slammed the door behind him and locked it. "Good God, Antonia! What the devil are you doing here?" he demanded, his eyes roaming her body, no matter how much he ordered them to behave.

She slid off the high bed, the action hiking his shirt up to mid-thighs.

Her sex was a shadowy triangle beneath the fine muslin, the split in the front dipping down, down, down her chest, exposing the sweet, tantalizing swell of her small breasts.

Lucas swallowed, his gaze snagging on her hard points of her nipples, which were clearly visible through the thin material of his shirt.

His legs, usually the sturdiest of limbs, suddenly felt wobbly. He leaned back against the door.

"Are you alright?" Antonia's brow furrowed with concern as she stepped toward him.

Lucas held up his hands. "No. Do not come any closer."

She stopped, a hurt look flickering across her face.

A brief pang of guilt stabbed him; he hated to cause her pain, but if she came too close, he'd fall on her like a starving man.

"What are you doing here? And why are you wearing my shirt?"

"What do you think I'm doing here?" she retorted, crossing her arms, a gesture which did nothing to cover her up, instead it pressed the fabric against her mouth-watering curves and served to lift the hem of the shirt an inch higher up her ridiculously long legs. "As to why I am wearing your shirt?" She shrugged, her gaze taunting and prim and sultry all at the same time. "Why? Do you want it back?" She uncrossed her arms and reached for the hem.

Yes! the untrustworthy voice inside his head shouted.

"No!" Lucas barked, again raising his hands in a staying gesture. "You can keep it," he added hastily, his blood thundering in his ears.

She smirked, visibly amused by his nervous behavior. Hopefully she was too innocent to recognize the raw, pulsing, consuming lust that lay just below the surface of his anxiety. Or the erection already pressing against his placket. Lucas wanted to toss her onto the bed and strip his shirt off her body so badly that he could taste it.

Thankfully, he did nothing of the sort. Instead, he gathered his wits and demanded, "You couldn't have been hiding in my cabin all the time. Where were you?"

"Do the details really matter right now?"

Lucas blinked at her tart retort. "No, they don't." He turned and strode toward the door. "I must go speak to my first mate. We will turn the ship around and take you—"

"Lucas, please don't."

"My God, Antonia! Of course I must turn around immediately. Your mother and father must be deranged with worry—"

"My mother already knows where I am."

"What?"

Rather than appear cowed by his bellowing, she fearlessly stood her ground. "Yes. In fact, sneaking onto your ship was my mother's idea." She hesitated and then added, "And it was Jonathan who told me I could hide in that large barrel in the wardroom until you were well away from Eastbourne."

"Your brother knows about this?"

Her lips twisted into a wry smile. "Apparently he discerned I was, er, infatuated with you four years ago. It wasn't until this visit that he suspected you returned my affections." She gave an unladylike snort. "It seems my brother is not as oblivious as I'd always believed. He was exceedingly pleased to help me get on the ship."

Lucas could only stare.

"As for my mother, well, she has known how I felt about you for years."

"And your father?" he asked in barely a whisper. "Has he known?"

"Er, my father—no, my mother doesn't think he has recognized any of the obvious signs that you and I were apparently exhibiting."

Lucas's shoulders sagged with relief.

But then she said, "He will know by now because my mother will have told him where I am, who I'm with, and why."

***

Lucas looked so adorably confused and frustrated that Toni wanted to climb him like a tree.

She suspected that now wasn't the time for such behavior, however.

"The baroness will tell Hugh that you've sneaked on to my ship?" he repeated, his eyes round and his expression appalled.

"Yes." Toni hesitated, and then added with a smile, "She will tell him once the Ghost is too far away for him to come after us. It was her advice that we go somewhere, marry, and present him with a fait accompli. She seemed almost certain that he wouldn't kill his own son-in-law. Almost."

He stared at her, unblinking and unamused

Toni sighed. "My mother gave me her blessing, Lucas. She said that trying to abide by society's expectations in matters of the heart was a recipe for unhappiness and that she and my father should be the last people to expect such a thing from me.

You must have heard about the scandal she endured when she married my father?"

"You mean because her first husband was Hugh's uncle?"

"Yes. Apparently, it was quite a transgression, and even now some people cut her acquaintance."

"That was over twenty years ago!"

"Yes, but the ton can have a very long memory. Even though their marriage wasn't against the law, it was considered unseemly." Toni waved the issue aside. "But the point my mother made was that sometimes a person must face unpleasantness and fight for their happiness."

Toni lowered her eyes and raked his magnificent body with her hungry gaze. And he was magnificent, the tanned muscles of his arms and chest gloriously showcased by his minimal attire. It had always amazed her that even in winter he often wore nothing more than breeches, knee boots, and a black jerkin that was made of tough boiled leather. He was the very image of masculine virility and just looking at him was arousing.

She forced her gaze back up to meet his. "My mother told me to seize what I wanted with both hands or I would regret my inaction for the rest of my life." Toni reached out and grabbed his bare upper arms—which were so big around it would take three of her hands to span one—her pulse speeding at the sensation of hot satiny skin stretched over rock-hard muscle.

His body stiffened at her touch, but he didn't move away.

"I am seizing you, Lucas. Because you are what I want." She narrowed her eyes when he just stared. "Why do you look so shocked?"

Still, he only stared.

Toni inhaled deeply. "I only have so much bravery left, Lucas So if you don't want me, then you need to tell—"

He moved like a predator pouncing on its prey, claiming her mouth with a wits-destroying kiss, his powerful arms pulling her tight against his hard body.

Toni closed her eyes and gave herself up to heaven on earth, praying that this time would last longer than the last.

Indeed, they might have kissed forever if not for the inconvenient need to breathe.

When they finally parted, Lucas said, "You are mad, Antonia—do you know that? And you have probably driven me mad because—" he broke off and shook his head, as if words were inadequate.

And then he lowered himself to one knee, and it was Toni's turn to gawk.

"Lucas? What are you doing?"

"I am honored that you want me—more honored than you will ever know. You are the only woman I have ever loved, Antonia." He took her hand and held it between his. "Will you do me the honor of becoming my wife?"

Toni knew it was unseemly to grin like a lunatic when one's beloved was on his knees waiting for an answer to his proposal, but she couldn't help herself. "Yes, Lucas. A hundred times, yes!"

Lucas's instant, joyous smile squeezed her heart. "You have made me the happiest and proudest of men. I will protect and cherish you for the rest of my life."

Her eyes filled with tears faster than she could blink them away.

"Why are you are crying, my love?" he asked, getting to his feet, his brow furrowed with concern.

"I am just so happy!" She gave a choked, watery laugh and flung herself into his arms.

Lucas caught her, holding her so tightly that she couldn't breathe. "You are mine, Antonia," he muttered into her hair. "Now and forever."

"Now and forever," she agreed, her face buried in his neck.

Lucas set her on her feet and cupped her jaw with one big hand. "You are so beautiful." He kissed her, but only lightly. "You are also far too tempting." He glanced down at her bosom, which she belatedly realized was shamelessly exposed by the V of his shirt.

"Tonight, you will sleep here while I bed down with the men."

Toni simply could not believe what she was hearing. Frustration and disbelief vied with the needy, demanding passion that had been simmering inside her for far too long.

When she merely stared, he went on, "Tomorrow we will—"

"Oh, I know what will happen tomorrow," she interrupted rudely. "You will approach my father, who may or may not choose to cooperate. If he doesn't, we shall have to waste time convincing and placating him. Even if he behaves graciously, we shall have to wait while the banns are read and it will take weeks."

"Er, well—"

"I can think of one sure way to convince my father to cooperate and to make him apply for a special license."

"What do you—"

Toni clasped the hem of the shirt, closed her eyes, and—before she could lose courage—lifted the garment over her head and tossed it aside.

For one long, terrible moment, the cabin was utterly quiet.

"Good. God."

She opened her eyes at the sound of his breathless and worshipful words.

His eyes roamed over her body and his lips were parted, as if he couldn't get enough air.

Toni had never been naked in front of anyone other than her maid, and the urge to cover herself was strong. But such cringing behavior would defeat the purpose of being brave in the first place.

So, she stood motionless and proud, as entranced with the changes in his appearance as he seemed to be with her body. His hands fisted at his sides and his massive chest heaved as if he'd been running.

Not to mention the transformation taking place in his breeches.

Toni stared shamelessly at the growing bulge beneath the worn, soft leather of his placket. Surely it could not be as large as it appeared to be.

Lucas gave a tormented grunt, and his palm settled over the front of his buckskins. He gripped the thick ridge and squeezed, the ropey veins and muscles of his forearm taut beneath the tanned skin.

"You are not making it easy for me to be a good man, Antonia," Lucas muttered, his eyes darker than usual.

Toni could see that a battle raged inside him as he stared at her, and she knew he was struggling to hold back

So, she took a step toward him, making his decision for him.

"Antonia," Lucas groaned, his restraint visibly crumbling as he reached for her, his work-roughened palms grazing her pebbled nipples, his huge hands dwarfing her breasts.

Toni whimpered at the exquisite sensation.

"My God, Antonia—you are perfect. Utterly perfect." He caressed her aching nipples, his expression a mix of adoration and desire.

Toni arched her back, thrusting herself wantonly into his hand. "Please," she whispered, not sure what she was begging for.

He made an almost pained sound as his hands closed around her, his touch tender yet firm, his hard, hungry look sending a spike of fear to her belly—fear that she would disappoint him. After all, Lucas was an experienced man, while Toni was an ignorant novice.

"Shhh," he murmured, obviously sensing her tension. "Take three deep breaths before you faint, love."

Only then did Toni realize she was holding her breath; small wonder she was dizzy. She inhaled deeply and let it out, repeating the action thrice more, until her head stopped spinning.

"Good girl," he murmured, rolling her aching nipples between his fingers until she was shivering and rubbing against him.

Just when she thought she'd burst out of her skin, his hands slid to her waist, leaving her breasts feeling heavy and needy.

Lucas made low, soothing sounds when Toni moaned at the loss of his touch. "We need to slow down, my love." His hands settled on her hips, his fingers gently caressing the sensitive skin of her pelvis. "I wish to give you pleasure, but I don't want to frighten or disgust you, Antonia."

"You couldn't—" she broke off, her throat too parched to choke out the words. Toni swallowed and licked her dry lips, his burnt sugar eyes tracing the movement, the nostrils of his sharp, high-bridged nose flaring. "You couldn't disgust me or frighten me, Lucas. And I know what happens between a man and a woman." She smiled. "You know that my mother and my naturalist brother would allow no one in our family to be ignorant about such matters."

Lucas chuckled, his severe expression lightening. "I'll wager Richard gave you one of those papers of his—the ones about the breeding habits of beetles?"

Toni laughed. "Yes, exactly so."

His expression once again became serious. "Are you a maiden, Antonia?"

"Yes," she said, her face flaming.

"Have you seen a naked and aroused man before?"

Toni briefly closed her eyes at his question, her face so hot the chilly cabin felt warm. When she opened them, he was waiting patiently. "I've seen drawings—in great detail—but no, I've not seen an actual aroused man."

"Would you like to see me or should I extinguish the—"

"I want to see you. I wanted to ask, but—" she broke off and shrugged.

"You should never hesitate to ask me anything, Antonia." He spoke the words firmly and gave her a stern look. "What you want is important to me—it is the most important thing to me."

She nodded.

"So," he said, taking a step back, his hand sliding from her cheek. "I am yours to command."

She ran her hungry gaze over his big body. His black leather breeches were so old they looked like tar poured over the thick muscles of his thighs. A band of pure muscle showed between the low waist of his breeches and the snug leather jerkin that fit him like a second skin, exposing his magnificent arms and a deep v of muscular chest. While he was handsome in his evening blacks, these clothes were Toni's favorite.

Before she could lose her nerve, she said, "I'd like to undress you."

His eyelids lowered and his hand, which had gone to the three ties on his jerkin, fell away. "I would like that a great deal."

Toni's fingers trembled as she reached for him. The leather was hot from his body and she fumbled badly before loosening all three ties and exposing the full glory of his torso to her gaze.

He was all ridged velvety brown skin, the thick hair on his upper chest narrowing to a thin line that disappeared beneath the waist of his low-slung breeches.

Toni laid a hand on his flat, hot belly.

He gasped. "My God, Antonia."

Her lips pulled into a smile as she caressed the muscles of his abdomen. "You're so hard here," she murmured, tracing the fascinating grooves and ridges with the tips of her fingers.

His belly tightened even more at her light touch, the muscles twitching beneath the taut skin. Toni gorged on him with her hands and eyes, stroking up his corded waist to his chest.

It was her turn to gasp when she nudged aside his vest and encountered two glints of gold.

"Oh my," she whispered, reaching for one of the little gold rings but then freezing and looking up.

He nodded. "You can touch them—it will bring me pleasure."

His words were almost as erotic as the sight of his pierced nipples, and her hands trembled badly as she reached out to explore the tiny nubs of flesh and gold rings.

Lucas hissed in a breath, the small discs of flesh puckering even more with each stroke of her fingers.

"Is this something many men have?" she asked, unable to pull her gaze away.

"No, I believe the custom originated in North Africa among some of the nomadic tribes," he said in a strained voice. "I've only seen a few sailors with these particular piercings."

Toni shivered at the thought of somebody putting metal through her breasts. They might be small, but they were extremely sensitive.

"Only men do this?" she asked.

"I have seen women, too."

Jealousy, hot and sharp, sliced through her. "You've seen them? T-touched them?"

Lucas laid a hand over hers, pressing her palm over his tight nipple. "I don't want to talk about other women, Antonia. Not now."

Why was she so jealous? She'd never felt even a twinge of jealousy about the Duke of Dowden, even though she'd known that he kept a mistress in London.

He took her chin and tilted her face until she had to meet his faintly amused gaze. "Why do you look so fierce?"

"Do I look fierce?"

He nodded.

"I was just thinking of you with other women, and I don't like it."

He lowered his mouth over hers and kissed her, this time more slowly and languidly; a tender, thorough exploration. When he finally pulled away, Toni was breathless and aching for more.

"You are my one and only love, Antonia."

She swallowed and nodded, the jealousy abating, if not disappearing.

Lucas shrugged his powerful shoulders, and the jerkin slid to the floor, leaving him bare from the waist up.

Toni thrilled at the way his formidable body flexed and tightened beneath her hands as she stroked and explored. She walked around him, wanting to see every part of him.

"Good God," she murmured, stopping behind him and dropping her hand when she saw his broad back. Toni knew there were scars because she'd seen them before when he'd worn the jerkin. But the worst of the scarring was down the middle of his back, the old welts going from the base of his neck all the way down into his breeches.

"They don't hurt, my love," he murmured. "Touch me. Please."

Toni blinked away the tears, not wanting him to know how much it hurt to see the mute evidence of all the pain he'd suffered in his life.

Her father might have kept the worst from his children when they were young, but as Toni and her brothers got older, he'd told them the truth of the brutal life he'd once lived. He, just like Lucas, had scars from his years lived under the lash.

But hearing about such brutality and seeing evidence of it were two entirely different matters.

Toni slid her arms around his waist and pressed her front to his back, covering him with her body while kissing his neck and shoulders, her hands exploring his taut, grooved abdomen up to his pierced nipples.

"Mmm, Antonia." He leaned against her and sighed. "This is heaven."

"I want you to show me what to do, Lucas. Please."

"You are doing very nicely, trust me," he assured her, groaning and arching his back when she tugged gently on the golden rings. "Harder," he whispered, his hands reaching back to grasp her hips and pull her mound against his muscular buttocks.

"Like this?" She lightly pinched the little nubs, smiling to herself when he hissed and ground his bottom against her sex.

"Mmmm, yes." He shuddered and then slowly turned. When he faced her, they were almost eye to eye. "Your hands are magical—too magical. You will have me spending in my breeches."

Her lips parted at his vulgar words.

"I'm sorry, that was crude."

"Yes—but I l-liked it."

He cocked one eyebrow. "Indeed?"

Toni nodded.

He flashed her a wicked smile. "Ah, you are a naughty thing, hmm?"

He sounded extremely happy about that, so Toni nodded again.

"That is fortunate, because you are going to marry a sailor, my love, and I will always be more at home on the deck of a ship than in a fancy dining room."

She twined her arms around his neck. "I want us to be together, Lucas—no matter where we are: a fancy dining room, the deck of a ship, or at my family's house." She swallowed. "And I want you to m-make love to me."

"You sound frightened."

"It's not that so much as—" she bit her lip.

"As what, love?"

"I'm just worried that I will not compare favorably to all the women in your past."

He made a dismissive clucking sound with his tongue. "Just looking at you is better than touching any other woman, Antonia."

Toni smiled, her fear melting at his words.

"Get on the bed," he murmured, walking her backward until her bottom bumped into the mattress. "Up," he said, lifting her with ease and then standing between her knees, which meant she had to open her legs.

Toni dropped her hands to her sex, covering herself.

He smiled at the gesture but did nothing to stop her. "I want to make this good for you, Antonia—so good. There are things I can do that will bring you pleasure and relax your body, so you will take me more easily."

He paused again, but she couldn't manage more than a nod.

"Some of them are shocking—at least to proper English ladies—and you—"

"Right before I was to marry, my mother told me about the things l-lovers do."

His eyebrows drew together at her confession, his expression suddenly thunderous.

Toni was more than a little startled by the savage look. "Are you—does it make you jealous to think of me marrying another man?"

He scowled. "I wanted to kill him. At first, because he would have what I had wanted for so long. And then because he was less than deserving. To think that a pig like that might have—" he broke off and shook his head. "I don't want to think about him, Antonia; I want to think about you. When you say your mother told you things, do you mean she told you about oral pleasure? About fingers and tongues and mouths on the most private part of a woman's body?"

Her face flamed, but she nodded and then added boldly, "And a man's body, too."

His eyelids lowered slightly, and his lips curved into a slow smile. "Yes, and a man's, too. Would you like that, Antonia?" he asked, his gaze hot and wicked. "Would you like to touch me with your mouth—your tongue?"

"Oh yes," she whispered.

"I have dreamed about you doing such things," he admitted, brushing a thick finger over her lower lip, prodding gently until she opened for him. When her lips closed around the tip, his eyelids fluttered shut and he muttered something she couldn't quite make out before opening his eyes and gently removing his finger, his expression one of regret.

"There will be time for that later," he said, toeing off his worn leather boots while his fingers made quick work of the two catches and four buttons on his breeches.

He bent to shove them down, obscuring her view for a moment before he stood and stepped out of his clothing.

Toni knew she was staring, but there was no way she could look away.

His organ jutted out straight and proud and was every bit as impressive as the rest of him. It was long, thick, and ridged with fascinating veins. The crown was fat and flared, but the shaft was even bigger around in the middle, the girth rather alarming.

Lucas took a step toward her, and her eyes jumped to his.

"I will not faint or scream," she assured him when she saw the notch of concern between his eyes. "I'm—I'm just very curious." Her eyes dropped again, as if pulled by an invisible force.

"Do you want to touch me?"

Toni was already reaching for him before he finished his sentence and they both gasped when her fingers slid around the slick crown.

She looked up and met his heavy-lidded gaze. "The skin is so soft."

His jaw clenched and his hand closed around hers and squeezed, the powerful muscles in his forearm flexing, a bead of pearly liquid sliding from the tiny slit.

Toni knew what such moisture meant, as she'd experienced it with her own body often enough when she thought about Lucas and became aroused.

"You want me," she whispered, joy and excitement fluttering in her belly.

"Yes, too much right now," he said with a tight smile. "I need to touch you, Antonia."

She didn't want to release him, but there was a need—a desperation in his eyes that she couldn't ignore. So, she reluctantly withdrew her hand.

"Move up on the mattress and lie back, love."

Toni scooted back and laid down, but not all the way; she wanted to watch what he did, so she propped herself up on her elbows.

Lucas set a hand on each knee. "Part your legs for me."

***

Antonia was every bit as delightful as Lucas had always fantasized, her wide, curious gaze making him so hard that he knew he'd never make it inside her before spending.

That was fine, because there would be plenty of time for that later. He smiled, warmed by the thought. Indeed, they'd have the rest of their lives to explore each other's bodies.

If Hugh doesn't kill you, first.

Enough, he ordered, banishing the inner voice if not for good, then at least for the night.

Lucas lowered his body to the bed, hissing when his aching cock rubbed against the cool counterpane.

"Part your legs for me, my love."

The muscles in her long, lean legs jumped and twitched.

"Shhh," he soothed, stroking up the silky skin on the inside of her thighs as she obeyed him, not stopping until his fingers delved into the reddish gold curls that hid her treasure.

He opened her with his thumbs, baring her delicate pink sex to his greedy gaze.

"Antonia," he breathed, blood roaring in his ears as he slid his fingers through her slick, swollen folds. He was delighted and relieved at such obvious signs of arousal; Antonia might be nervous about what was going to happen, but at least she wanted it.

Lucas lowered to his elbows and then buried his nose in her sweet slit, inhaling until his lungs felt like they might explode.

The sound of her startled laughter pulled him from his ecstasy, and he raised his eyes to hers as he slowly and deliberately licked her engorged bud with the flat of his tongue.

"Lucas!" she cried out as her hips jerked.

That was all the encouragement he needed, and he covered her sex with his mouth, tonguing her fleshy nub while gently sucking.

His Antonia was not shy when it came to her pleasure, groaning and writhing and making enough noise that she would likely be heard in the officers' cabins.

Lucas brought her to the brink of pleasure three times, teasing and licking and sucking, but always stopping just before she could orgasm.

"Lucas." Antonia gave him a sulky, heated glare and spread her thighs even wider, the wanton, erotic gesture making his cock throb.

He couldn't help smiling against her tender, swollen flesh, thrilled by her openly sensual nature. And when she lifted her hips to grind her sex against his face, he didn't tease her. Instead, he tightened his lips on her tiny bud and sucked.

She came fast and hard, shuddering and crying out his name while coating his tongue with her sweet juices. Her first climax had barely finished when he coaxed a second, more powerful orgasm from her.

Lucas gave her time to recover, leisurely kissing, licking and sucking his way to her entrance. He breached her tight opening teasingly at first, barely flicking the point of his slick tongue into her, until she pushed up onto her elbows again and made increasingly frustrated and demanding whimpers.

Their gazes locking as he mimicked the sexual act with his tongue, sliding deeper with each thrust, her hips lifting to take more of him, grinding her delicious cunt against his face and soaking his nose, mouth and chin with her arousal.

Lucas circled her engorged nub with his thumb as he fucked into her, penetrating her over and over until she once again exploded on his tongue.

He was so intent on her orgasm that his own climax caught him by surprise, his aching balls clenching and his untouched shaft thickening before he realized what was happening.

Half-blind with need, Lucas drove his hips into the bed, shooting jet after jet onto the counterpane, some part of his mind distantly amused and embarrassed by his juvenile performance.

Once the last spasm had passed, he allowed himself a moment to rest, laying his face on the softness of her inner thigh as he reveled in his happiness. No matter what happened when he faced Hugh, at least he no longer had to suffer in silence—to want without hope. After this night Antonia was his and nobody could take her away from him.

Smiling at the thought, he took a deep breath and pushed himself up.

Antonia gazed up at him with slitted eyes, lazily tweaking one of her tiny, pebbled nipples with the fingers of one hand.

Christ. Her sensuality was so innocent, unschooled, and natural that he felt the impossible happen—his cock attempting to twitch back to life.

But as much as he yearned to bury his length inside her, his lover looked ready to drift off to sleep.

"All is good?" he asked, tucking a lock of hair behind her ear.

Her lips curled into a satisfied smile. "All is very good," she said and then yawned, her heavy lids lowering and her stroking fingers stilling.

Lucas watched as she drifted off to sleep before stealthily moving off the bed without jostling her.

Once he'd covered her and dimmed the lantern, all the negative thoughts he'd barricaded in their cell earlier began banging on the bars, demanding to come out so they could hector and shame him for betraying his dearest friend.

Are you really going to run off and marry Hugh's daughter like a sneak thief?

Do you truly believe he will forgive you if you do what Antonia suggested and present him with a fait accompli?

And so forth.

The voices berated him while he used a damp cloth to clean up the mess he'd made on the bed.

And they berated him some more as he pulled on his breeches, shrugged into his jerkin, and pushed his feet into his boots.

Not until Lucas had gone up on deck and informed his first mate about his sudden change in destination did the voices finally leave him in peace.

Chapter 8

T oni was having the loveliest dream. She was with Lucas and they were naked and he was looking at her with the most delicious combination of love and desire and he was touching her and—

Her eyes popped open as every muscle in her body suddenly tensed.

"Lucas!" she cried out as the pleasure exploded, swamping her with wave after wave of bliss.

As Toni floated toward consciousness, it took her a moment to realize that it hadn't been a dream at all. Instead, it had been a hot, wet mouth with a sinfully wicked tongue.

A low growl vibrated through her body, soft lips teasing and stroking. "Open wider for me, Antonia." His big hands closed around her thighs and Toni let her knees fall open like the eager wanton she was.

"Such a good girl," he muttered, his breath hot against her spread sex. "I'm going to make you come until you scream."

And then he did exactly that, working wave after wave of almost excruciating bliss from her, until she couldn't bear any more.

"Please Lucas," she gasped, squirming and squeezing her thighs shut, clamping around his head hard enough to earn a muffled laugh.

He gave her over-stimulated bud one last lingering suck and then prowled up her body on his hands and knees until he emerged from the blankets, his lips red and slick, his eyes heavy with lust.

Toni suddenly remembered last night, and how he'd done the same thing and given her endless pleasure but taken none for himself—at least not in the way she knew men had their release.

"I'm sorry about last night—I must have fallen asleep."

"Why are you sorry? You were delightful." His lips curved wickedly. "And delicious."

Toni squirmed, both pleased and embarrassed by his naughty teasing. "But you didn't—I mean, you never—"

He captured her mouth, his tongue thrusting between her lips and stroking into her with suggestive motions.

She jolted when she realized what she was tasting.

He chuckled when she pulled away. "You taste how sweet you are?"

"You are so wicked!" Toni placed her hands on her face, which felt like it had been burnt by the sun.

Lucas smirked, well-pleased with himself as he ran a trail of kisses to her ear, which he nibbled, something hot, long, and hard rubbing against her lower belly.

"Oh, you're—" she bit her lip, not sure of the least embarrassing way to say he was aroused.

"I am," he agreed, his hips pulsing gently, rubbing his slick shaft against her sensitive stomach.

Her mouth opened, but no words came out.

"Yes, my love?" He pulled back slightly, his eyes almost black as he looked down at her.

"Can we—I mean, will you put yourself inside me?" she asked, her face scalding as she uttered the scandalous words.

"Are you sure?"

She swallowed and nodded, out of words.

"It will hurt—even though I will go slowly."

One look at Lucas's, er, instrument told her it would probably hurt a great deal—at least at first. But she ached for him.

"I want you, Lucas. I want to be yours, utterly and completely."

He growled and flung back the bedding. Toni's lips parted, and she stared, rapt. His body was hard and kissed by the sun, his shaft thick and long; he was raw masculine perfection.

And he was hers, finally.

He reached between her sprawled legs and stroked her slick, swollen folds with a confidence that was almost as arousing as his erotic touch.

"You see how excited you make me, Antonia?"

Toni took his question as permission to stare at his erection, which was hard and jutting, the fat crown slick with his desire.

He was truly the most gorgeous thing she'd ever seen.

He gently probed the entrance to her body with one finger. "Are you ready?"

Toni nodded, her gaze darting from his face to his manhood to the hand between her thighs.

Lucas pushed inside her slowly, the stretch surprising, but not uncomfortable.

His jaws tightened. "You're wet, but so damned tight. Can you relax your muscles, Antonia?"

It was strangely easier said than done, but after a moment, he nodded. "That's good," he murmured, pumping into her.

Toni gorged on the sight of him while he worked her harder and deeper. Without realizing it, she lifted her hips, taking him even deeper.

"More?" he asked.

She nodded, biting her lower lip when he eased a second finger alongside the first.

"Breathe, my love." He smiled and nodded as she relaxed around him, employing his thumb on her sensitive peak and working her toward a climax so quickly it was almost embarrassing.

"So beautiful," he murmured as Toni arched off the bed, digging her heels into the mattress and lifting her hips to take him deeper.

Before she came all the way down from the heights, he slid his fingers from her body and lowered his torso over her, pressing his blunt crown against her opening.

"Don't become tense—try to relax," he said, sounding more than a little tense himself. "I will fit—your body was made to take me."

She thrilled at his words, even though it hurt to take him.

He was big and felt twice as large as he looked.

Just when Toni was about to ask him to stop, he gave a low, almost pained grunt. "I'm in all the way. My God, you feel like heaven, Antonia."

His words eased any discomfort she was feeling. He was inside her. And it surpassed every expectation she'd ever had: the man she loved was inside her body.

She reached up and took his face in both hands, his skin scratchy with his night beard, the black hairs mixed with silver. "You are the only man I have ever loved or wanted." She tilted her hips, and he hissed as he slid in a bit deeper.

"I love you, Antonia," he whispered.

And then he began to move and all thought fled.

***

Antonia was as tight and sweet as Lucas had known she'd be. But it was more than just her virginal body he loved. It was the generous, indomitable woman inside. She was young, but she was a woman who knew her own mind, and she'd wanted him, so she had taken him.

And thank God for her strength and firmness of purpose. It horrified him to think that if not for Antonia's determination, he would be sleeping in his bed alone, probably dreaming of her and how they would never be together.

Their gazes locked as he pumped into her, fucking her with deep but gentle strokes, her eyes blazing with unfettered emotion as she gazed up at him.

Lucas loved Hugh like a brother, but he loved Antonia more. How could he have ever thought to sacrifice her happiness for any reason? Especially one like male honor or society's notions of respectability?

Although he was the son of a whore, had once been a slave, and could not trace his lineage back to the Conquest, Lucas would make her happy.

"I love you so much, Antonia," he said, meeting her gaze as he reached between their bodies and teased one more climax from her.

Only when she was bucking and writhing beneath him did he hilt himself and give into his need. "You're mine, Antonia," he whispered as his shaft pulsed inside her and he filled her with his seed, chasing his own bliss into oblivion.

Epilogue

December 27th

Several Days Later…

L ucas's black eye had mostly faded by the morning of the wedding and Toni's father had stopped scowling at his son-in-law almost as soon as the vows had been spoken and the vicar had pronounced them man and wife.

Well, he'd almost stopped scowling—at least at Lucas. Right now, he was scowling at Toni, his single green eye boring into her.

Toni couldn't help thinking that her father looked especially piratical as he leaned close to her and said in a low, menacing voice, "Duke says you are insisting on going with him."

Toni glanced across the cozy sitting room to where the wedding guests had gathered after their sumptuous breakfast feast, to where her husband of approximately four hours and forty-one minutes was standing between Toni's eldest brother Lucien—the Earl of Davenport—and his wife, Phil. There was a sprig of mistletoe above their heads and Lucas was smirking indulgently as Luce kissed his wife of over ten years as if they were lovebirds about to embark on their bridal journey.

He must have felt Toni's gaze because he turned to her, his eyes sliding to her father and then back to her before he lifted his eyebrows, his look saying: do you need rescuing?

Toni smiled but gave a slight shake of her head; she could easily manage her father and was almost delirious with happiness that he'd stopped glaring at poor Lucas.

When she turned away from her husband and back to her father, she saw he looked even more irritable, as if he'd seen their exchange.

"I am going on this next journey with Lucas and on any other journey he takes, Papa, so you can huff and puff all you want, but it will make no difference."

"You know there have been several pirate attacks along that route, don't you?" he demanded, ignoring her as if she hadn't spoken.

"Yes, Papa."

Hugh Redvers gritted his teeth. "Are you even going to listen to reason?"

"If you mean am I going to listen to you on this subject, then no. If my husband"—Toni experienced a shiver of delight at the word— "believes it is safe to take me with him, then it is safe." It was Toni's turn to scowl when she saw the way her Papa was now glaring at Lucas. "And I won't have you browbeating him on the subject."

He opened his mouth to retort, but before he could say anything, Toni's mother drifted up beside her husband.

"Are you browbeating our daughter, Hugh?" the baroness asked with an amused twinkle in her brilliant blue eyes.

"I'm trying to talk some sense into her, Daphne, but she refuses to listen." He heaved a huge, put-upon sigh, but finally said, "She is right about one thing: she is her husband's concern now."

"God save the poor man," a wry voice said behind Toni's shoulder.

"Very droll, Richard," Toni said, elbowing her second oldest brother in the side hard enough to make him yelp.

"Children, behave yourselves," Richard's wife Celia murmured as she drifted up beside her husband and jerked her chin toward the group of adolescents only a few feet away. "We want to provide an exemplary role model for our children, don't we Sir Richard?"

"Don't look at me," Richard said. "She started it."

Toni snorted, and Celia rolled her eyes.

"Have you noticed how they gang up on us more and more often?" Richard asked Toni's father.

"I wonder where they learned that from," Hugh said dryly, cutting his wife an accusing, but affectionate, look.

But the baroness wasn't paying the conversation any attention. Instead, she stood on her toes and then kissed her husband on the cheek.

His single eye went round at his normally decorous wife's public gesture of affection.

He raised a hand to his cheek. "What was that for?" he asked. "Not that I'm complaining."

The baroness pointed up.

Toni's father glanced up and then laughed before turning to Richard. "Good Lord! How many of these things did you hang up?"

Richard smiled smugly. "I'm not telling."

"Sixty-one," his wife said.

Everyone laughed.

Richard shrugged. "If something is worth doing, then it's worth doing well."

The conversation moved on to other matters and away from Toni and Lucas's upcoming bridal journey and she breathed a sigh of relief. She adored her father, but he really could be like a dog with a bone. At least he was over his anger at Lucas when it came to marrying his only daughter—surely irrational as it had been Toni who'd all but forced her husband into proposing—and the two men were already showing signs of being closer than ever.

"Is everything alright?" Lucas murmured when he came up beside her.

"Everything is fine," she whispered, "but I doubt he's finished just yet."

Although her father could not possibly have heard her, he turned away from Martin Bouchard—who'd just joined their group—and gestured to Lucas. "Talk some sense into him, Martin. Tell him not to take my daughter on such a dangerous journey."

Bouchard's unusual golden eyes twinkled with amusement, and Toni was grateful when he gave Lucas a look that said he understood. "There have been problems on that route," the handsome Frenchman admitted mildly, "but I will take Sarah on that same journey in the spring."

Hugh flung his hands up in the air. "Traitor!" he accused, but not with much heat.

Lucas cleared his throat. "I appreciate your concern for Antonia, Hugh—she is precious and I would never put her in danger." He glanced down at her, his eyes so full of love it still left her breathless.

Toni knew Lucas would prefer not to take her into such a politically volatile part of the world, but she'd always yearned to visit North Africa—not unusual after growing up with a father and his friends who all spoke of the region—and now was as good a time as any.

Not to mention the fact that it would be Lucas's last journey, but they'd not told her father that yet, although Toni's mother was in on their little secret.

Lucas lifted an eyebrow at her, and Toni nodded, biting back a smile.

He cleared his throat and said, "Antonia and I have an announcement to make."

Everyone stopped talking and turned.

Lucas slid his arm around Toni. "This next voyage will be my last as captain of the *Batavia's Ghost*."

Surprise rippled through the room.

Lucas ignored it and turned to the baroness. "Thanks to the generosity of my mother-in-law, Antonia and I will move into Whitton Park after we return from this journey."

There was a stunned moment of silence, and then the room erupted with noise.

Toni grinned as she accepted congratulations from friends and family.

"It's perfect, Toni," Richard murmured into her ear, giving her a kiss on the cheek. "We'll all be together this time next year—permanently." Richard and his wife were moving their family to a manor house only three miles away. It would be beyond perfect to have all her brothers around her. Well, all except one… "

Predictably, it was her father who asked the question: "Who will captain the Ghost, Duke? I hope you're not just handing her over to anyone?"

Lucas grinned at Jonathan, who looked fit to bursting—it had taken bodily threats to get her younger sibling to keep mum about his momentous news.

"Jonathan?" Her father gaped for a moment and then grinned so hard his face threatened to split in two. "Why, that's marvelous!"

Lucas led Toni away from the noisy celebration, guiding her over to the relative quiet by the window. He smiled down at her and pointed above their heads.

She laughed at the ubiquitous sprig of mistletoe above them and kissed her husband of only a few hours.

When she pulled away, Lucas said, "I think it all went well."

They both turned to where her father was smiling, slapping Jonathan's back, and saying something in a decidedly boastful tone.

"I think it went wonderfully," she murmured, glancing at the longcase clock and wondering how long they needed to play cards tonight before they could decently sneak up to the bridal suite.

"Antonia, look," Lucas said.

She turned to see he was pointing out the window.

"It's the first star of the night." He gave her a tender smile. "When I was a boy, we used to say they were lucky for wishes."

Toni suddenly recalled the wish she'd made the evening she'd been gathering garland and marveled; could it really have been less than two weeks ago?

"Antonia?" Lucas asked. "Don't you want to make a wish?"

She smiled up at him. "I've already got everything a woman could wish for."

Sometimes, Toni thought as her husband claimed her mouth with a second, far more passionate kiss, wishes really did come true.

Dearest Reader:

I hope you loved Antonia and Lucas as much as I did. I have to admit this novella was a lot LONGER (yeah, you KNOW how I like to write looooong) but I had to hack and cut it down to an acceptable size to include it in the DUKE IN A BOX anthology last year. Maybe someday I will republish this novella with considerable expansions, but for right now my publisher contract prohibits a full-length novel on any of the characters from THE OUTCASTS series so I have to be content to give Antonia a novella.

Don't worry, if I ever do add more stuff to the novella I will "refresh" the book rather than republish a whole new book, which means you will get any new changes without having to pay more money!

If you've read the other books in the series, you might be wondering about some of the time-line stuff in this book, which doesn't match up exactly. Yes, I had to fiddle and fudge it a bit to get the story I wanted. That is one of the perks of being an author in control of your own world, lol.

Many people ask if I will ever write a story about any of the other characters from this particular "world" and I'm happy to say that *yes*, I definitely plan to write books for Adam and Mia's (from ***DANGEROUS***) other two daughters as well as Gabriel's best friend from ***NOTORIOUS***, Lord Byer. I'm not sure when these will come out, but they are certainly floating around in my head.

Right now I'm working my way through ***BALTHAZAR: THE SPARE***, which is a lot of fun because the story is set during the Victorian Era, which I adore reading about but rarely write about. This is another "family" series which I've decided is my favorite.

In addition to being asked for more novellas and novels about the characters in ***THE OUTCASTS*** and ***THE REBELS OF THE TON*** I've been asked more than a few times for extended epilogues. This is a very interesting idea to me and I am intrigued. If I did that, I'm not sure which series I should do first? The two I mentioned above or one of my other series—like ***THE MASQUERADERS***? If you have an opinion on that concept, please let me know what you think at: minervaspencerauthor@gmail.com.

In the meantime, I hope you are having a safe and happy Spring 2023 and that you've been blessed with oodles of wonderful books.

Until next time, take care and happy reading!

Minerva/S.M.

About S.M. & Minerva

Minerva is S.M.'s pen name (that's short for Shantal Marie) S.M. has been a criminal prosecutor, college history teacher, B&B operator, dock worker, ice cream manufacturer, reader for the blind, motel maid, and bounty hunter. Okay, so the part about being a bounty hunter is a lie. S.M. does, however, know how to hypnotize a Dungeness crab, sew her own Regency Era clothing, knit a frog hat, juggle, rebuild a 1959 American Rambler, and gain control of Asia (and hold on to it) in the game of RISK.

Read more about S.M. at: www.MinervaSpencer.com